Hope you
Erica & Jaime's story.
Amy Stephens

Falling for Him

Amy Stephens

The Falcon Club Series: Book One

Falling for Him
The Falcon Club Series: Book One

Cover design by Amy Stephens
Image courtesy of Depositphotos / Prometeus
Interior formatting by Amy Stephens

Chapter One

AS I STOOD IN LINE to register for my upcoming classes for the fall semester, I couldn't help but notice the different types of people I'd be having them with. The women were dressed in tailored business suits with their high-heel Manolo Blahniks while the men wore their Armani suits with matching ties.

I looked down at my sparkly Toms and wiggled my toes, knowing my feet were more comfortable than the lady's standing directly in front of me, who continued to shift her weight from one side to the other. Sadly, I stuck out like a sore thumb, while she blended in with the others.

We'd been standing in line now for the past hour, slowly advancing forward. I hadn't tried to start a conversation with anyone simply because they all seemed to be caught up in their own worlds, chatting away on their phones or handling business on their iPads and tablets. Yes, I may have been on my phone too, but I was browsing through my Facebook page. These people probably didn't even know what that was.

And something else that bothered me, they were all older than me. Some of them could easily be friends with my parents. I knew the chances of me running into any of my former high school classmates were pretty slim, but from the looks of it, I'd be the *only* one there from my high school. I guessed that could be a good thing. Did I really want my friends knowing I was going to school *there* instead of away at State like I'd talked about nonstop my entire senior year? And the chances of finding a cute guy to date? Well, the possibilities were slim to none from what I'd seen so far. I could just see my parents' faces now if I brought home one of the guys who waited in line like me. Um, no. Not happening. If they were a year or two older than me, maybe, but these guys were more appropriate for my mother.

Two people advanced, and I noticed someone had opened another computer station at the registration table. Now, instead of there being six, there were seven people typing away on their computers, entering all the registration information just so we could move on to the next station. The line was moving, and that was the important thing. The sooner I could get out of there, the better off I was.

No matter how hard I tried to like it, I still had a bitter taste in my mouth about this university. It wasn't so much that the school itself was bad. In fact, it was known to be a pretty damn good one, but it just wasn't what I'd planned for my freshman year of college to be like. Bishop University was more for working adults, and I still wanted to enjoy and experience college life to the fullest, just like my friends.

You see, everything about my first year of college had been planned since I'd entered my senior year of high school. My best friend, Monica, and I had been so excited that we'd be attending State together. Before graduation, we'd toured the campus and picked out a cute little two-bedroom apartment we'd planned to share, and had even picked out the classes we were going to take together the first semester. We were all set to enjoy our freshman year of college, just the way it was supposed to be. All my plans for the fall came crashing down the week after I graduated high school.

My parents thought it'd been cool to make this big announcement that they were getting a divorce. Yes, a divorce. My sister, Beth, and I were floored by the news. Neither of us had seen that coming and still, four months later, really couldn't understand why our parents couldn't stay together any longer. It happened, I know, but it wasn't supposed to happen to *my* parents.

The divorce had taken place regardless of what we'd thought and there was nothing Beth or I could do to change the way our parents felt about one another. According to them, they just didn't love each other anymore. Why couldn't they have waited until after I'd moved out? Why did it have to happen just as I was getting ready to live out my college dreams? My sister was hardly going to be affected by this since she was still in middle school, but I, on the other hand, didn't deserve to have all my plans destroyed. *I wasn't the one getting divorced.*

It was decided that my mom would get an apartment closer to the city and to her job and my dad would keep the family home that was just on the outskirts of town. Beth and I were free to stay with either parent anytime we wanted since we'd have rooms at both places, but there was more to the story than what I saw on the surface. At this point, I really didn't care to know what or who had caused them to suddenly "fall out of love." I wanted them to fall back in love, or at least, pretend they loved each other so we could keep our family together and not have it ripped apart.

In the end, the divorce turned quite ugly instead of the nice way our parents had explained it to us in the beginning and accusations started being thrown at one another. Before long, I couldn't tell which parent lied or told the truth, and it was evident that all my plans for the fall were now just a thing of the past. Nothing was going to change that.

The money that had been put aside in my college fund was used to pay for lawyers and legal fees and, in the end, if I was going to attend college at all in September, I needed a new plan. I couldn't depend on my parents to assist me with preparing for my future while they were still fighting with one another. To make matters worse, my mom decided to change jobs to one that paid substantially less right before the divorce was finalized. I'm sure her lawyer was just trying to get more child support and alimony for her instead of looking at what was happening now.

So, instead of moving away to State with Monica, there I was enrolling in Bishop University. I really shouldn't be so upset about it. I mean, I was still going to college, after all, but this definitely wasn't the school I'd had in mind. By going to school there I was able to still live at home and work my part-time job. I wasn't excited about the student loans I had to take out, but going this route would save me money in the long run. After all, according to what my parents tried to convince me, it didn't matter where my degree came from. The certificate was the same regardless of the university I attended.

Bishop was geared more to the student who was already in the workforce with a good job, just looking to get a promotion or make a career advancement. Most of the students were married with families of their own and needed a college schedule to work around their already busy lives. I didn't exactly "fit" that criteria, but it was either Bishop or no college at all.

I might have felt a little better about going there if I saw someone close to my own age, someone who was fresh out of high school, but so far, I was out of luck. Whether I liked it or not, the most important thing was that I was getting an education.

"Next."

Someone lightly tapped me on the shoulder, and I turned around to see what they wanted. I'd been so wrapped up in my thoughts I hadn't noticed the open slot at the table in front of me.

"You're next up," the gentleman said as he pointed in the direction of the available representative.

"Oh, I'm sorry," I mumbled and slowly walked over to the table.

I handed my printout to the lady, and she placed it down beside her computer monitor as I tried to get comfortable in the chair.

"Good morning," she said rather pleasantly.

"Morning."

I had to get out of this mood I was in before everyone around me noticed. The last thing I wanted people to think was that I was a bitch or something. I'm really not, but I just need to find something that makes me happy again.

The registrar busied herself behind her computer, typing in all sorts of information. I was amazed at how quickly she typed. The printer behind her started to spit out paperwork, and she slid her chair back to retrieve it. She grabbed a pen from the cup holder and then marked the different areas I needed to sign. Once I was finished, she handed me more paperwork and told me to look everything over then proceed to the next line.

I couldn't believe I'd waited all that time in line just to sign a few times and be directed to yet another line. I glanced down at the paperwork and noticed the page on top had suggested classes I should take for my first semester as a freshman. Of course, English 101 was listed along with Western Civilization, but why would it suggest Principles of World Religions, Introduction to Philosophy, or Introduction to Geology? None of those even sounded remotely interesting or pertained to my degree in Business Management.

It was pretty broad, but I'd figured once I got a couple of my core business classes behind me, I'd be able to narrow it down to a more specific program. I was really looking forward to taking my first business class this semester too, but, according to their recommendations, it didn't look as if that was going to be happening. I knew these were suggested classes for me, but hopefully my advisor would see those weren't really related to business and he'd suggest something else.

I could only hope.

I pulled out my phone again and picked up where I'd left off, browsing the statuses of my friends on Facebook.

Ten minutes had passed when the door opened and two men walked out. An older man dressed in a military uniform turned to shake hands with the other gentleman, who I assumed was the advisor, before he walked away. I'd never been around anyone in the military before and, for some reason, just seeing him intimidated me. It wasn't that they frightened me or anything, but seeing the decorated formal uniform gave off a different vibe than the customary camouflage I was used to seeing in the movies or on television.

"Hi, I'm Dan McDonald and I'm going to be your academic advisor," he said as he walked toward me. I have to admit he appeared pleasant and sounded friendly enough, but he wasn't at all what I'd expected my advisor to look like. "Welcome to Bishop."

I extended my hand to shake his, and then followed him into the room. He shut the door behind us and instructed me to take a seat in one of the two chairs that surrounded his desk. I noticed he had several degrees framed and lined up on the wall, and I couldn't help but wonder if they'd come from Bishop. On his desk were a couple small picture frames, but I wasn't able to see who the pictures were of. No doubt, they were probably photos of his wife and kids, because he didn't appear to be old enough for grandkids yet.

Dan asked me a little about my high school classes and why I'd chosen Business Management as my field of study. He didn't ask anything personal about why I'd chosen to attend Bishop, and for that I was thankful.

Next, he told me the classes he recommended for entering freshmen. I cringed when I heard him say the exact same ones that were suggested on the paperwork.

Damn it! Those were not the classes I wanted to take. Who in their right mind would want to take geology, philosophy, or world religions?

As I finished marking the choices, I realized it could be much worse. I could be stuck taking classes in one of those technical institutes you see advertised on television for massage therapy, or how to cut hair. Yes, that could be me, but thank goodness it's not. I'm going to force myself to like this school even if it kills me.

In the end, I decided on the usual entry level English and history classes, world religions and Introduction to Geology. I really tried to squeeze in a literature class, but English 101 was a prerequisite and couldn't be taken simultaneously.

As Mr. McDonald typed my class selections into his computer, he informed me I was the last one to enroll in the world religions class. It was officially full and closed to any more students. I didn't know if I should've been jumping for joy or squalling just then, but this day hadn't turned out to be what I was hoping for at all. He handed over my actual schedule, and if I had no other questions or changes, I was to sign at the bottom and keep the top copy for myself.

I kindly shook his hand and then stood to walk out of the room.

"Ms. Kennedy, two of your classes are located in the building across the street, while the other two are located on the military base that's just a couple miles down the road. You shouldn't have any trouble locating it, but you'll need to take your schedule down to the base and have them issue you a temporary ID card and base pass."

I felt so overwhelmed I couldn't even comment. Military base? ID card? What had I gotten myself into? I thought I'd be going from building to building on a regular campus, not driving across town. Just one more reason not to like it there.

"Excuse me, but did you say military base?" I questioned, not sure if I'd heard him correctly.

"Yes, ma'am. Bishop has a joint education policy with the United States Air Force. Many of the military personnel are students at Bishop and earning their degree just like you. In fact, the gentleman who was here before you just signed up to obtain his second degree with us."

"Oh, I see." I really hoped Mr. McDonald didn't hear the disappointment in my tone.

"I can understand your fear of going to the base. You'll find other students there as well so there's nothing for you to worry about. We're very fortunate that Bishop has this partnership with the Air Force. It's a benefit for the students as well as for the military."

I mumbled thanks to Mr. McDonald and then closed the door behind me.

I walked out to my car and fumbled in my purse for my keys. I pulled out my wallet, checkbook, and cell phone and still couldn't find them. I patted my pockets, even though I never put them there, and then leaned over to look inside the car. There, on the front seat, were my keys. *As if this day couldn't get any worse for me.*

I called my mom to bring me the spare set from home and sat on the curb next to my car to wait for her. Right then, I just wanted to be angry with the world. A few months ago, I'd had a great life. Now, I wondered if going to college was even the right thing for me. I was only going to be miserable taking classes I really didn't want to take in the first place, and now I had to go to the military base too. What next? Would it be smart to find a second job, save up all of my money and join Monica at State for the second semester? Maybe I could even go back and take out more money on my student loan. Starting in the winter wouldn't be so bad, would it? I mean, after all, I'd be at State just as I'd wanted to be from the very beginning.

Since I had nothing better to do while I waited for my mom, I pulled out my schedule and glanced over it again. I had English and history on Monday and Wednesday nights with geology and world religions on the other two nights. What kind of college offered classes only at night? How was I supposed to keep up with my favorite television shows? On the bright side—if there was one—at least I'd have my Friday nights off and I wouldn't have to get up at the butt-crack of dawn for an eight o'clock morning class as I probably would have had to do at State. What good was a free Friday night without my best friend being there?

I placed my chin on the palms of my hands and propped my elbows up on my knees. I could already feel it now. This was going to be a long semester. I was so miserable I didn't even bother to call Monica to tell her about my classes as I'd said I would. I just wanted my mom to hurry up and get there with my keys so I could go home.

Chapter Two

AS BADLY AS I HATED to admit it, the first night of class wasn't so bad. There were about twenty-five people in my English 101 class and I, of course, looked to be the youngest. The instructor started out by telling everyone she understood when "real life" happened and she wouldn't hold it against anyone who made it to class late or had to skip altogether.

I couldn't believe what I was hearing since I'd always thought that most instructors frowned on tardiness and hated for their classes to be interrupted once they had begun their lectures. Don't get me wrong, the teacher wasn't saying it was okay to purposely be late, but she understood when traffic was bad, when work required you to stay late, or when your babysitter cancelled at the last minute. Now, if the other classes ended up being that way too, I might start to have a different opinion of it there. Wait until I shared *that* with Monica!

She was already jealous of my class schedule because, as an entering freshman at such a large school, she'd gotten a couple early morning classes when all of mine had started at five in the evening. I'd finally broken down and called her over the weekend, and she couldn't believe how lucky I was to be having classes at the Air Force base. Her reaction had been the complete opposite of my own.

"You are so lucky," she'd told me. "You're going to be in class with a room full of hunky military men."

Not knowing if that was really going to be the case, we'd joked about swapping places with each other. To humor myself, I kept thinking about those gorgeous guys from the movie *Top Gun* and wondered if maybe she was right. Maybe I had ended up with the better end of the deal. We'd see after tomorrow night when I'd venture out to the base for the first time.

As for tonight's class, though, there was nothing "gorgeous" or "hunky" about any of those classmates. There were no Tom Cruises, and the only thing "hot" was the lady in front of me, who was apparently experiencing a hot flash. She kept fanning herself with her notebook for most of the class. No, that was not my idea of "hot."

Going around the room, each student took a turn stating their name and briefly sharing a little something about themselves with the class. Most of the students had been out of school for many years and were coming back to either finish their degrees, or begin a new one. While most of them did appear to be close in age to my parents, there were a couple students who'd just graduated high school within the last couple years. I did feel a little better by the time class dismissed, knowing my classmates were serious about their studies and not just attending to appease their parents.

Our first assignment was made, and I found myself eager to get started on it. Since I was taking four classes, I needed to stay on top of things and not put them off until the last minute, as I was known for doing back in high school. Going out and partying were priorities back then, but not so much the case now. I'd already made up my mind that I wouldn't be looking for a boyfriend, either. Judging by what I'd seen so far, cute guys were nonexistent there, so why not focus more on my grades. As for finding a boyfriend, well, I'd have to look elsewhere.

Since my boss had to rearrange my work schedule around my evening classes, I was only able to work a couple hours during the day now. So much for that theory of saving money for college. I'd barely be making enough to cover food and gas. The trendy boutique inside the mall did most of its business during the evening and on the weekends, and since there were already a few girls working the weekend shifts, my availability left plenty of time for homework.

On the drive home, I called Monica and we chatted for over an hour. I missed her so much and was jealous of all the new people she'd met so far, including the good-looking guy in her science class who she'd been paired with. Monica was even planning on asking the guy out once she got to know him a little better, if she even waited that long.

I didn't even want to discuss the students in my class. If I became remotely interested in any of them, it'd be with one of their sons and not them.

No. I didn't want to go that route, either.

I made my way upstairs to my mom's second-floor condo. No one was home yet so I fixed myself something to eat. My sister, Beth, came in a little later from being next door at the neighbors' and we chatted for a bit before I turned in for the night. Mom had gotten in the habit of coming home later than normal, and neither Beth nor I bothered to wait up for her anymore. We were pretty sure she'd started seeing someone already, and we really didn't want to be placed in the middle once Dad found out.

The next day at work was crazy. One of my co-workers decided to call in sick, so we were short staffed. Between the manager and me, we did our best to take care of business, despite getting hectic at times.

I glanced down at my watch and noticed it was already after four o'clock. *Shit!* I had less than an hour to get to class out on the base.

My plan had been to leave a few minutes early to allow myself plenty of time to get to there. Me, always the worrier, still felt uncertain about going to the military base. And there I was, running late.

With both my classes tonight being on base, it sucked that I was running behind and that I'd left my schedule printout at home. I couldn't remember the classroom numbers and wasn't exactly sure which of the buildings I'd need to find.

My mind drew a complete blank.

On the day I had my ID card made, the officer had given me directions for the building I needed, but I'd failed to write them down.

Why me? I seriously doubted I'd get lucky and that tonight's instructor wouldn't frown on tardiness, either.

I wished I could've changed into something more comfortable, but my black skinny jeans, V-neck sweater, and open-toe booties would have to work tonight. I wouldn't really be overdressed since so many people came to class straight from work wearing business attire, but after wearing this outfit all day, I was ready for my oversized t-shirt, yoga pants, and flip-flops.

Pulling up to the guard gate, I flashed my ID at the gentleman just as I'd been instructed to do. He noticed my school sticker in the front window and saluted me. The gate arm lifted, and I pulled forward. That had been easy enough, but I wished I'd taken the time to ask him for directions. Just seeing him in his military uniform caused my stomach to feel queasy. I'd eventually adjust to seeing guys in their dress uniforms, but until then, I'd just have to deal with the nervousness until it subsided.

I drove around a couple blocks, careful not to get too far from the main entrance in case I got lost. Nothing seemed to resemble classrooms, though.

Just when I was about to give up, I noticed a guy jogging on the side of the road I'd just turned down. After turning back around, I pulled up beside him and rolled my window down. At first, the guy didn't hear me because he wore earbuds and listened to his iPod. He removed them when he noticed I'd slowed down.

"Excuse me, but I seem to be lost. I'm looking for the Bishop University building. Could you possibly point me in the right direction?" Thank goodness that guy was dressed in a normal t-shirt and running shorts, and not his military apparel, or I'd never have been able to stop.

Hold on a minute.

Damn, if all the guys on this base were as hot as that one, my semester may have just gotten a little bit better. I needed to stop looking at the uniform and focus more on the individual. There might be hope for me, after all.

"Of course, ma'am. Just go straight ahead to the four-way and take a left. It's two blocks down on the right."

Ma'am. He called me ma'am. He flashed me a killer smile, and I could feel my cheeks blush.

"Thank you. I really appreciate it."

As I pulled away, I glanced in my rearview mirror at him. He cut across the street, and I eventually lost sight of him. I sure would have liked to have caught his name.

I couldn't believe I'd let myself get so easily distracted like that. Time was of the essence, and I needed to focus so I could find my way. I couldn't worry about a good-looking guy jogging down the street, sweat dripping from his body, running shorts over those toned legs…okay, you get the idea.

I made the turn just as he'd said and there was the campus building over to the right. Bishop University Campus was written just above the main entrance in big, bold letters. I felt like an idiot for not being able to find it on my own.

I pulled into the parking lot out front and made a couple loops, looking for an available space to park. There were several spots up near the front of the building right next to the handicap parking, but they all had signs stating they were reserved for certain military officials.

Frustrated, I pulled back out of the lot and then up behind a small compact car that had parked next to the curb along the side of the street. Hoping it was okay to park there, I grabbed my bag and headed for the entrance.

I looked down at my watch. I was officially ten minutes late for class. God, I dreaded walking inside the classroom. The last thing I wanted was for everyone to turn and stare at me. I was sure the instructor would probably ask for my name, and I surely didn't want to be singled out in front of the entire class. *Please, just let me slide in at the back of the room and take a seat in the rear. I promise I won't be late again.*

Since I'd left my schedule at home, fortunately I remembered the name of the instructor and looked for it on the board in the front lobby. Thank goodness for it since there was no one seated at the information counter.

Jordon 202.

Rather than wait for the elevator to get to the second floor, I took the stairs in search of room 202. I was prepared to see about twenty or so students, similar to that of my English class, but what I found when I opened the door was more like fifty, and every single seat looked to be occupied. Then I remembered what my advisor had told me about being the last one into the class. *Ugh.* I prayed this would get better.

The door hinges made a terrible squeak as it closed behind me, and all heads immediately turned to look in my direction. *No sneaking into this classroom, that's for sure.*

I made a quick glance around, hoping I could spot a chair to sit in, but there was nothing available. Rather than cause another scene, I slid in behind the back two rows of tables and walked over to the right side of the classroom, careful as I stepped around everyone. I placed my bag onto the floor up next to the wall, and then pulled out my textbook. It weighed a ton, so I propped it against the window ledge long enough to pull out my notebook and a pen. Before I could do anything else, I accidentally bumped the oversized book, sending it crashing to the floor. The sudden, loud noise startled everyone and all heads, once again, turned to look at me. No doubt, I was getting good at getting everyone's attention tonight.

I felt my face redden, and I couldn't stand to see everyone turn around and stare at me yet again. Quickly, I kneeled and took a seat directly on the floor. Hopefully, the instructor would allow a break between the first and second hour of class and I'd be able to apologize for coming in late and disrupting the class.

Not really able to see very much from my view from the floor, I looked around the classroom and noticed the majority of the students were men. Some were dressed in their standard military attire of dark blue slacks with a lighter shade of blue shirt and super shiny black shoes, but there were also several dressed in dark gray jumpsuits too. I wondered why they were dressed differently, but figured they must be part of some elite group there on base. For all I knew, maybe these were flight suits or something. I tried not to stare, but there were a couple of them who were absolutely gorgeous. I was surprised to see so few women taking the class but, like me, they probably hadn't been keen on this particular subject, either.

I struggled to hear what the instructor said and found myself flipping through the pages of the textbook. A few of them had creased when the book had fallen so I tried to fold them back in place. I'd paid too much money for it to start looking tattered now.

The more I looked through the book, the more I found myself dreading this class. The subject matter just didn't appeal to me at all. I never knew there were so many types of religions throughout the world.

The gentleman sitting in the seat closest to me passed a copy of the syllabus over and I jumped, not expecting it. Had I been so caught up in my book I hadn't heard the instructor say something directed toward me?

I nodded to thank him for the handout.

I scanned over the front page and couldn't believe all the expectations of this class. I realized it was a general studies class, but it wasn't as if it was going to really be beneficial to my major. There were so many projects, essays, and exams listed I really wondered if I'd made a mistake in selecting this over one of the other choices. Was it too late to go back and change it?

Chairs shuffled across the room, and I looked up to see several of the students stand and head toward the door. They left their things on top of their desks, so I assumed this must be a break and not the end of class. So much for thinking it could be over already.

I stood and stretched my legs. Just as I bent down to grab my things from the floor, I noticed the instructor walking toward me.

"Nice of you to join us," he said as he stopped right in front of me.

He was dressed in jeans and a button-down shirt, not at all what I'd expected for a religious class. I guess, in my mind, I'd expected to see someone dressed in a suit or something more appropriate for church on Sunday since it was, after all, a religions class. He was probably in his late fifties and had a receding hairline.

I extended my hand. "Hi, I'm Erica Kennedy. I'm so sorry for disrupting class earlier. I had a situation at work, and then I had trouble finding the building once I made it on base."

"I understand. Glad you could make it. I'm Professor Jordon. Did you get the class syllabus I passed back to you?" I noticed his forehead wrinkled when he spoke.

"Yes, I did. Thank you."

"Since I covered it first thing and you weren't here yet, read it over, and if you have any questions, see me after class. I'll be glad to go over anything with you."

I was appreciative of his offer. Considering there were so many students in his class, I was sure he hated having to repeat himself multiple times, and had limited time for one-on-one discussions.

"I will. Do you know if there are any more seats available? From what I could see, they all appeared to be taken." I hated having to ask about something as simple as a seat, but I couldn't sit on the floor for the remainder of the class.

"Once everyone returns from their break, I'll see what we can do, Ms. Kennedy."

I felt really silly standing in the back, holding my things while waiting for class to begin again. I watched as everyone made their way back inside and to their seats. It was obvious the guys wearing the gray jumpsuits hung together so they must be some top-secret group. It was too bad they didn't mingle with the others, but maybe the group didn't allow it. I didn't see any women wearing the jumpsuits, either. Maybe they had secret rules or something. Who knew? I spotted a handful of people in regular clothes, and while we were of the minority, it felt good to see two of them were females. The ratio of men to women in the class was interesting, and if we were putting dibs on anyone, I'd like to know more about the ones in the jumpsuits. Ha!

The classroom was laid out with rows of tables placed together with two chairs per table. Since the class was so large, some of the tables had squeezed in a third chair and it made them look cramped. Once everyone was finally seated, Professor Jordon brought an extra chair from out of the corner and placed it at the end of the second row. One of the guys wearing a gray jumpsuit stood and motioned for me to take his seat. *Score one for me, huh?*

I slid in behind everyone on that row and then walked to the seat he'd offered. He slid over the next chair, and everyone in the row shifted until we were all seated comfortably with enough room between us.

"Thank you," I told him as I placed my bag and purse underneath my chair. It was nice of him to make room for me.

His gaze met mine, and for a moment, I felt as if it sucked me in. His eyes were a deep chocolate-brown that almost looked black against his pale white skin. His dark hair was slicked back and secured at the base of his neck with an elastic band.

I found that a little interesting since I wasn't aware of the military allowing guys to have ponytails. It wasn't a long ponytail since it stopped just at the top of his shoulders, but when I looked around at several of the other men dressed just like him, I noticed they too had similar hairstyles and not the buzz cut that was traditional of the military. Maybe this wasn't a military group, after all. Unless they were a secret service group disguised as someone else when they went out on a mission. I'd have to look more into that.

The guy appeared to be in his late twenties or just slightly older, and from what I could tell, he looked to be extremely physically fit. His upper arms bulged underneath the jumpsuit's short sleeves, and they left me to wonder what the rest of his body must look like underneath his clothes. His shoulders were broad, and if I leaned just slightly to my left, I'd be able to touch him. The suit wasn't too snug, but it clung to his body in all the right places. I was so caught up in his appearance I hadn't noticed class had already started back up again.

Professor Jordon directed the class to open their textbooks to Chapter One, and then he began lecturing. I flipped open my spiral notebook and then immediately took notes since I'd missed out on what was said in the first hour of class. I found myself sneaking glances over at ponytail-jumpsuit guy, and I was thankful he'd been nice enough to make room for me to sit. Not everyone had been so generous.

My fingers cramped from all the notes I'd written, so I placed my pen down for a moment. I opened and closed my hand a couple times to work out the stiffness, then wiggled my fingers before I picked up my pen again.

To my surprise the guy lifted his notepad and angled it so I could see the couple notes he'd taken during the brief time I'd had my pen down. That was nice of him to share his without me asking, and I needed to make sure I thanked him at the end of class. I scribbled the word "thanks" at the top of my page and pointed to it. That would do for now.

He nodded as he glanced over to see what I'd written. He smiled, showing a perfect set of teeth. As I smiled back, I noticed there was something written on the front left pocket of his jumpsuit. I couldn't make the words out from the angle I was sitting, but I became curious to know what it said. I made it a point to find out later.

Professor Jordon stopped his lecture from the textbook and handed out more paperwork pertaining to our first project assignment. I was thankful for the moment to put my pen down since I wasn't used to note taking at such a rapid rate. It'd never been that way in high school.

I leaned up in my seat and stretched my arms out in front of me. Propping my elbows on the edge of the table, I glanced out of the corner of my eye and tried to make out the writing on the pocket of his jumpsuit without being too obvious. Curiosity was getting the better of me. I could make out some kind of symbol or image in the middle and in a half-circle shape just above the picture were the words "Falcon Club."

Hmm. I wondered what kind of club that was. While I wasn't familiar with the military or any of their programs, I still figured it must be some private club or organization, and the guys were allowed to wear those outfits in place of their traditional clothing. It still didn't explain why several of them had ponytails, but I liked looking at them nonetheless. I'd never dated anyone with long hair before since the preppy kids I'd associated with back in school were all into the trendy look, but I could possibly do the ponytail thing.

Was I being for real? Just looking around, I could see all those guys were older. I mean, the one next to me easily had ten years on me, give or take, no matter how good he looked, and the others were at least the same age as him or older. No, I needed to stick with guys my own age. With my little bit of "experience," there was no way I was putting myself out there for an older man to laugh and make fun of me once he realized just how young I was. He might have been nice in offering me his seat, but that was as far as I was going to go with that. No, no, no. Nothing more.

After the teacher made it back to the front of the class from passing out all the paperwork, he instructed everyone to pay close attention while he read through the assignment. There would be two parts to this project, one that involved individual work and the other that involved group work. He went on to explain that groups would be assigned at the beginning of the next class, and we would be allowed to briefly introduce ourselves prior to starting the project. We would have some class time devoted to the group part, but it was expected of us to meet outside the classroom for the remainder of it. Not only did the school have a library on their main campus, but we would also be allowed access to the military library. He emphasized that using the military one would eliminate any obstacles we might run into. I wasn't sure what he meant by that, but we shouldn't be lacking for information that was for sure.

Honestly, I wasn't looking forward to the group part since I didn't know one person in the class so far, but hopefully that would change, and I'd be placed with a group that was willing to work hard. I thought about Monica and her lab partner and wondered if I'd get lucky too. I looked around the room. Nah, I doubted it.

Once there were no more questions pertaining to the project, the instructor started back on his lecture. I kept stealing glances at the jumpsuit guy and wondered what my chances were of being placed in the same group with him.

I could hear the conversation with Monica now. "You should see the guy who I'm doing group work with," I'd tell her. "He's part of the Falcon Club." She might have the guys in fraternities to look at, but I had the ones in the Falcon Club.

Class finally ended and I stood to collect my things.

"So, what do you think of the class so far?" jumpsuit guy asked me. He spoke with a slight Spanish accent, and I loved the sound of his voice. It wasn't deep or anything, but the words rolled off of his tongue, making him sound exotic.

"I'm…I'm not sure just yet." I couldn't believe I'd just answered his question like that. "I mean, the workload seems to be pretty heavy, but I'm sure I'll manage."

"I've not seen you around before. You must be new," he continued, obviously interested in what I had to say since he'd not made an attempt to leave yet.

I nodded. "Yeah, this is my first semester at Bishop. How about you?" I immediately wanted to slap my forehead. With this guy being in the Falcon Club, he'd probably been taking classes for quite some time now. Blame it on me being young and asking stupid questions.

"This is actually my last semester," he quickly added.

"Oh?" I hoped he didn't detect disappointment in my voice.

"Yeah, I found out I was one class shy of graduating and needed an elective. This class seemed interesting enough."

I kept thinking back to how much I'd frowned upon the class selection and there this guy was finding it *interesting*. I guess for him, being one class away from finishing, anything would be interesting.

"Doesn't sound like it's going to be an easy class with all the projects we've got lined up," I added, trying to prolong our conversation as long as possible.

"I've had Professor Jordon in another class before and he's a pretty good instructor. Likes to make the class fun. That's part of the reason I selected it."

"I hope you're right. I've got a full load this semester and don't want to start off on the wrong foot."

"Well, if you need anything, just ask."

He winked and gave me another one of his killer smiles before walking towards the door.

I thought I was going to melt before we made it out of the classroom. He was an absolute babe! While I hadn't thought about looking for a ring, it wouldn't surprise me to find out he was married. Someone as good looking as him either had a gorgeous wife or a long line of women trailing after him. I made a mental note to find out more about him the next time we were in class.

"Thanks for the offer. I really appreciate it." I called out to him. "See you next week."

"Likewise."

Before I could make it out the door, I ran right smack into one of the chairs. I caught myself before tripping over it and making yet another fool of myself. Once outside the building, I paused long enough to take a deep breath. Just that little bit of conversation with him had sucked the life out of me, but in a good way. There was no denying I was interested in finding out more about him. Older or not, he was pretty damn hot. And his accent just added to the icing on the cake.

Cars pulled out of the parking lot, and I wondered what kind of vehicle my jumpsuit guy drove. I hated that I hadn't gotten his name, and I immediately started going through possible names in my head, wondering if I could guess correctly.

Thankful my car hadn't been towed because of where I'd parked, I got in behind the wheel and then looked around to see if I could spot him. I hoped I hadn't sent him the wrong message. I didn't want him to think I was boring or immature, but how was I supposed to act around an older man? I noticed several of the guys who wore the jumpsuits had huddled together on the sidewalk as though they were waiting for something. And there he was. I spotted him, standing right with them. I could have picked him out anywhere. Whatever that group was they all seemed to be cordial with each other, and I was determined I was going to find out more. I needed to come to terms and get over this slump I was in from being there. I might be jealous of Monica and all the friends she was making, but I could make friends too. And if they happened to be older, oh well. At least they were nice to look at.

I looked up to see headlights coming toward me. A big bus, similar to that of a Greyhound or Trailways, pulled up next to the curb and then opened its doors. I couldn't help but stare when all the jumpsuit guys slowly walked up the bus's steps. That just made it even more mysterious. *Just exactly who were these men and why were they traveling by bus*?

My jumpsuit guy was the last one to climb onboard, and catching me by surprise, he lifted his hand to wave at me. I almost felt like sliding down in the seat because I hadn't even realized he'd watched me walk out to my car. I was mortified he'd caught me staring. I had no other choice but to wave back.

I cranked up my car and then pulled away before the bus had a chance to leave first. I admit, I was curious to see where the bus was headed, but I'd had an interesting night already and didn't need any other issues.

As I drove through the security gates leading away from the military base, I couldn't get him out of my mind. I kept seeing that gorgeous smile of his when he'd looked at me. The words he'd spoken kept replaying over and over in my brain. His accent could drive any woman wild.

Later that night, I called Monica and told her all about him.

"Men in uniform are so freaking hot," she told me.

"I know, but this was a different kind of uniform. And he had long hair that was pulled back in a ponytail."

"Are you serious? Maybe the military is changing, but who cares. If he's hot and he's checking you out, go for it, girl."

"Oh, Monica, I don't even know his name. He could be married for all I know. Or even gay, for that matter." I couldn't help but let out a little laugh. I honestly didn't think someone as attractive as him could be gay, but you never know these days.

"Well, looks like you've got some work to do."

"Yeah, yeah. We'll see."

Images of my jumpsuit guy filled my mind all through the night. The next morning. I actually found myself looking forward to going to class instead of dreading it. I just had to make it to the following week so I could see him again.

Chapter Three

THE FOLLOWING TUESDAY I MADE sure to leave work with plenty time to get to class. There was no way I was going to show up late again and cause another scene.

I wore my favorite pair of skinny jeans with a printed top and my favorite pair of Toms. My outfit was cute but still comfortable. I remembered from last week that the handful of non-military civilians in the class had been dressed casual for the most part, but I didn't think shorts or yoga pants were the appropriate thing to wear. The idea was to look nice and not draw too much attention to myself, even though I did want a certain someone to notice. I wondered if he'd be dressed the same way tonight or if he'd wear something different.

I walked into class and found many of the seats already taken. I wasn't sure if we were taking the same ones we'd had last week or if it was whoever got there first got to sit where they wanted. Regardless, with the class being so large, getting a seat early was important.

I glanced around to see if I could spot him. *Did I really want to sit next to him again*? Of course I did. I had, after all, spent extra time picking out my outfit and straightening my hair.

Looking down at my watch, I noticed there was still ten minutes before class started, and it looked as though he wasn't there yet. Or, if he was, he wore something different than the jumpsuit and I just hadn't been able to pick him out amongst the others.

I walked up toward the second row of seats where we'd sat before and found a seat that left an empty spot on either side of me, just in case. Hopefully, he'd show up soon and notice the empty seats before they were taken.

The professor walked in, and after saying hello to a few of the students, walked to the podium at the front of the room. I pulled out my notebook and pen and then glanced back over my notes from last week. The classroom became quiet and everyone looked toward the front. There were quite a few empty seats still left, unlike last time.

Professor Jordon did a quick overview of Chapter One, since we'd covered it last week, and wasted no time beginning Chapter Two. With both seats still unoccupied on either side of me, I felt disappointed my guy hadn't shown up tonight. Without completely turning around in my chair to look, I realized no one who'd worn the gray jumpsuits were present, which explained the extra empty seats. I felt relieved knowing he hadn't dodged sitting next to me.

Roughly fifteen minutes into the lecture, the instructor paused when the classroom door opened and about fifteen guys walked in. I turned around to look and my gaze went straight to him. They were there, the men in jumpsuits.

I felt my face flush as he walked toward the second row of tables and headed my way. He'd remembered our seats, after all.

I shifted uncomfortably when he placed his books onto the table. I think it was more nerves than anything. He fumbled around with his notebook, and then patted his pockets. What was he doing? Suddenly, it dawned on me. He was looking for something to write with.

I leaned down and pulled a pen out of my bag that was on the floor propped against my chair. I offered it to him, and he smiled appreciatively. Thank God I had a spare one.

Thank you, he mouthed, and I nodded. Just watching his lips form those two little words sent chills throughout my body. There was no doubt in my mind that I was attracted to him.

I hadn't realized Professor Jordon was lecturing again, and hoped I hadn't missed anything important. For the next hour, I took note after note. No matter how hard I tried to focus and pay attention, my mind kept drifting to him. Yes, *that* him.

Once the first hour of class was up, we were dismissed for a fifteen-minute break. Chairs scraped across the floor as everyone stood and headed to the door. I grabbed my purse and figured I'd go to the restroom. It wouldn't hurt to glance in the mirror just to make sure my hair and makeup still looked okay.

My jumpsuit guy went to the front of the class and had a one-on-one conversation with Professor Jordon. I looked back at him before walking out the door, and he looked up just in time to see me leave.

After I was finished freshening up, I reapplied my lip gloss before walking out of the restroom. Just as I stepped out the door, I almost ran right smack into him.

"Oh, I'm sorry," I managed to say, embarrassed that I'd nearly ran him over.

"My bad. I hadn't realized you were in there." *Who was he trying to fool*?

His accent sounded even sexier tonight than it had the first night of class.

"By the way, I'm Erica." I stuck my hand out to shake his and prayed I'd completely dried my hands. There was nothing worse than shaking someone's hand that was damp, even if it was due to it just being washed.

I was proud of myself for not stumbling over my words. He was just so mouth-watering to look at.

"Nice to meet you, Erica. I'm Jaime."

He extended his hand, as well, and I felt as if he held mine just a bit longer than he should have. I almost felt as if he was about to kiss the top of it, but changed his mind at the last second. I really wouldn't have minded the gesture, but I supposed doing that at school probably would get some looks if anyone watched.

"Well, Jaime, it's nice to meet you." Dear God, I hope he hadn't detected the giddiness in my voice. *Was I that obvious?*

"Thank you for the pen earlier. I guess I must have dropped mine on the way here."

"No problem. I usually try to keep extras." You better believe I'd toss in a few more just in case the situation arose again.

Students began heading back inside the classroom, and I was sad to end our conversation so soon. Hopefully, we'd pick back up again when class was over.

He held the door open for me to enter first, and I went to my seat. I kept repeating his name over and over in my mind. *Jaime. Jaime.* He'd pronounced it as "hi-may," so I was pretty sure he was Hispanic, thus explaining his accent.

The next half of class, Professor Jordon covered the group assignment more in-depth, and then called out names. I held my breath, listening carefully. Sure enough, Jaime and I were placed in the same group along with Hector, who also wore a gray jumpsuit, and Ray, who sat just two chairs down from me. Ray was dressed very professional with his fancy name-brand suit, and didn't look too thrilled to be placed with us.

I looked over at Jaime, and we both smiled. I was glad to be placed in the same group with him and I felt his smile showed he felt the same way, too. I seriously hoped that was the start of *something*. Apparently, something about me had changed, because the Erica I thought I knew would never have started crushing on an older guy. No way!

After all the groups had been announced, we moved our chairs around one of the tables, and Jaime sat on the same side as me. Our legs lightly brushed against one another, and I felt the heat coming from his body. The second time they touched, I didn't bother to move mine away. It felt natural and I left it at that.

We each took turns briefly introducing ourselves, but I felt it was still too soon to get very personal just yet. It was on the tip of my tongue to mention the Falcon Club and the gray jumpsuit, but I held back from saying anything.

Ray took over as being the head of our group and immediately read over our assignment. He appointed different topics that we all needed to research individually, then on Thursday night we planned to meet at the library on base. Since I already had my pass and ID, Ray assured me I'd have no trouble getting into the library as well. Plus, it was convenient for everyone in the group. Ray and I both had classes from five to seven on Thursday, and it shouldn't take but a few minutes to meet with Jaime and Hector shortly thereafter.

Hector asked Jaime a question in Spanish, and I immediately felt intimidated because I had no clue what they said. Jaime smiled at me, and then looked back at Hector. Hector nodded, and while I wanted to say something about it being rude, especially because I felt he'd said something about me, I just looked back down at my papers and pretended it didn't really bother me.

Jaime must have sensed my uneasiness because he reached underneath the table to lightly squeeze the top of my leg. It took me by complete surprise, but I kept my hands on top of the table, not sure how I should react to that gesture.

Ray pointed out a couple other things we needed to work on, and once we felt comfortable with the assignment, we were all free to go for the evening. I gathered up my things and then stood to push my chair underneath the table. I was still bothered by whatever Jaime and Hector had said, even though I didn't have a clue what it could have been.

"You leaving already?" Jaime asked, and I could tell by the look on his face he didn't want me to go.

Hector stood and brought his fingers up to his lips, indicating he was going outside to smoke.

"I'll catch up with you shortly," Jaime told him, and Hector walked out the door. Ray didn't bother sticking around, so the two of us sort of lingered around in the classroom. A few other students were still there as well, so we weren't really alone.

Something about Jaime was so intriguing, and yet I couldn't quite place what it was. He was hot as hell and not someone I would typically be interested in, but he was gorgeous and I wanted him. Yes, that was correct. *I wanted him*.

Now that I was in college, what was wrong with looking at older guys? Maybe dating someone a little older than me might be what I needed to branch out.

Jaime scooped up his things then followed me toward the door. We walked out to the hallway together, and several people looked our way and stared. Did we look that mismatched? A few other guys wearing the jumpsuits were huddled together in their little groups, talking amongst themselves. Some looked up at us, while others paid little or no attention to us at all. I pretended not to notice. We eventually reached the exit and the man who sat by the door checking IDs gave me a cold, hard look when I placed my hand on the door.

What was that all about?

The last time I was there he'd been really nice, but the feeling I got from his stare tonight kind of gave me the creeps, almost as if I were doing something wrong.

Jaime and I continued making small talk, but it was mostly about the class and the assignment. We stopped just at the edge of the sidewalk. I spotted Hector talking with a brunette woman at the end of the building, obviously deep in conversation with her. The lady passed him another cigarette, and then placed the lighter up to his mouth so he could light it.

Jaime noticed me watching them and told me they were friends.

"Oh. Okay. She's not in our class is she?"

"No. I think she's in another one."

I'm not sure why it mattered. They were obviously adults, so why should I care that they were talking, unless there was something more to the two of them than I was aware of. Still, it was none of my business, so I looked away. I wanted to bring up that I didn't appreciate Jaime and Hector talking about me in Spanish, but I decided against it. You better believe if it happened again, though, I'd voice my opinion about it.

"So, what are your plans after graduation? You did say this was your last class, right?" I tried to be nosy without being too obvious.

"I'm not sure what I'm going to do. I've thought about attending graduate school, but I'm not sure my family could afford it right now."

"Would you enroll here? I've heard they have a decent graduate program."

"Yes. Even if the classes I needed were downtown at the other campus, the bus still provides a shuttle service for us. If I did enroll in graduate school here, I wouldn't be able to complete the program before having to leave."

I was confused. First of all, why would he still have to take the bus? Why not drive himself? And secondly, what was the part about leaving before completing the program? It didn't make sense.

Just when I was about to inquire more, I heard the sound of the bus pulling in. Several of the guys heard it too, and walked over to the edge of the curb. I was sad, knowing he had to leave.

"I guess you're leaving with them?" I asked, and pointed to the other guys who were now boarding the bus.

"Yeah, I've got to go. But I'll see you Thursday night, right?" he asked.

"I'll see you then," I replied.

And just like that, he stepped onto the bus. I didn't want to look silly standing there watching him as he walked down the aisle in search of a seat, so I casually headed to the parking lot to my car. I did manage to quickly look back, but the bus was already pulling away.

Chapter Four

ON THURSDAY NIGHT I PULLED my wallet from my purse as I drove up to the guard gate at the base entrance. I flashed my ID to the guy and recognized him from being on duty the last time I'd been there. I think he recognized me, too, because he barely even looked at my identification. He was young and cute, but didn't do much else for me. Right now, my sights were set on Jaime.

Jaime and Hector had given me directions to the library, which was only a couple blocks over from the Bishop classrooms. Hector said he used the library quite often so he'd save us all a table on the second floor. As soon as my Geology class had ended, I rushed out to my car so I wouldn't be too late getting there.

Since I'd never visited the military library before, I had no idea what to expect. I hadn't needed to use the main campus library yet, but I had been told the military library was a top-notch facility and was, hands down, one of the best. There were plenty of cars in the parking lot, which surprised me, being this late in the evening, but Hector had said we'd be able to stay until ten o'clock.

I walked inside and couldn't believe how huge it was. I spotted a sign for the elevators and walked over to push the button to take me to the next level. Once inside, I was shocked to see there were buttons for five floors. I pushed the one for the second floor, and the elevator slowly made its climb. When the doors opened, I stepped out and looked around. There were rows and rows of shelves filled with books, in addition to lots of tables with computers. Several people occupied the terminals and paid no attention to me. I noticed a help desk just off to the side, and a young lady looked up as the elevator door shut behind me.

I turned to the right and figured I'd look around for the guys in my group before I sought help locating them. Walking past several more rows of bookshelves, I noticed even more tables, some with computers and some without. I heard voices, and when I turned the corner, there was Ray and Jaime. Several books were already spread out on the table before them.

"Hey, guys. I got here as quickly as I could." I dropped my things onto the chair next to Jaime.

"Hi, Erica."

I loved hearing him say my name. I noticed the slight curl of the corner of his mouth as he spoke and I wondered if he was as excited to see me as I was him.

Stop it! I told myself. I needed a quick reminder that we were there to work on a project and nothing else.

Ray looked up and finally acknowledged me by tilting his head to the side. He had a pencil tucked behind his ear and his glasses were positioned low on the end of his nose. I hadn't noticed him wearing them in class before, so I wondered if he chose to wear them just for tonight. He came across as annoying with the way he presented himself to others, so it wouldn't surprise me if he'd just worn them for show.

Ray was very serious about our assignment, so I didn't waste any time catching up on the information they'd already researched. I was serious about it, too, but I wanted to be relaxed and not rushed as Ray made me feel. Maybe that wasn't just an elective class for him and was the reason he seemed to take it so seriously. Either way, I planned to do my fair share of the work just as everyone else.

"Where's Hector?" I asked.

At first, I thought maybe he just hadn't arrived yet or he was in the restroom, but Jaime quickly spoke up, saying that Hector wasn't going to make it tonight. Judging by the scowl on Ray's face, I knew this was obviously a sore subject they'd previously discussed before I'd arrived, so I figured I'd ask Jaime about it later.

After an hour of intense note taking and reviewing some material Ray had already printed off for us, I leaned back in the chair. I was tired, but we were already making good progress for the first time meeting.

I heard a vibrating sound and realized it was Ray's phone. I hadn't even thought about putting mine on silent prior to arriving at the library and was thankful it hadn't rung. Ray reached for his and excused himself from the table to take the call.

Jaime looked tired, too, and I'd admit, I was ready to call it a night. I'd been going nonstop all day since early that morning, and had briefly stopped at midday for a quick bite to eat. I'd gone straight from work to class, not having enough time to eat dinner, and I was starting to feel my stomach rumble. I was hungry and wondered if there was anything close by to eat. Not wanting to embarrass myself with a growling tummy, I thought about looking for a water fountain. If I could get a few swallows, it might satisfy my hunger pains for a little while longer.

"Do you know where the bathrooms are?" I asked.

"I think they're back by the elevator," Jaime replied.

"I'm just going to step away for a moment while Ray's on the phone. I'll be right back." I felt him watching me from the moment I stood from our table until I was out of his sight. I thought about turning around just to double check, but I wasn't sure how I'd react if he had been staring.

Jaime was right about the bathrooms being near the elevators, and sure enough, there was a water fountain halfway between the men's and women's doors. Before returning to our study area, I glanced at myself in the bathroom mirror. My eyes looked tired and my hair was starting to look a little frazzled, so I finger combed it to add a little bit of texture to it. I pulled some lip gloss from my purse and then reapplied it to my natural pink-colored lips. Before walking away, I sprayed a light mist of my favorite Victoria's Secret body spray that I always kept in my purse. *Why on earth was I concerned about my appearance and the way I smelled right now?* Seriously, it was late at night, and that was the last thing I should be concerned about. *Who cared what I smelled like, right?* Or was it because I wanted Jaime to notice?

I walked back to our study area, and Jaime looked up at me with just a hint of a smile. *Damn!* He'd pulled the elastic band from his hair and it was now hanging loosely just below his shoulders. I couldn't get over how shiny and healthy it looked, and I wanted nothing more than to be able to run my fingers through it. I was glad to know I wasn't the only one who was concerned with their appearance.

Ray still hadn't returned so, instead of sitting back down, I stood next to Jaime as close as I possibly could without touching him. He flipped through some pages of a book that wasn't related to our assignment. At that moment, I realized I couldn't care less about the project any more tonight, and I hoped Ray felt the same way when he returned. I was beyond tired and hoped he'd just go ahead and leave so I could spend some one-on-one time with Jaime before the library closed.

Jaime stood and walked over to one of the nearby couches. I followed and sat first, surprised by how comfortable the couch was for it being in a library. It wasn't as hard and stiff as I'd anticipated. He followed suit and sat with less than a foot separating us.

"How long have you been here on base?" I asked, eager to find out a little more about him.

Jaime hesitated a moment before answering, as though he thought carefully before he spoke. "I've been here for five years. I was at another facility down in South Florida before being transferred."

He was somewhat vague with his answer, but I just assumed whatever he did pertaining to the military was probably top secret and he wasn't at liberty to discuss very much. I didn't pry, and he didn't volunteer much more.

"What do you do when you're not busy with work and school stuff?" I hoped I didn't come across as being nosy, but I needed to know more about him. I thought back about whether or not he was married and played around with the idea of how to broach the subject with him. I played it safe and looked down to see if he wore a ring. I was relieved to see he didn't have one on. It didn't mean he wasn't, but it still made me feel better not seeing an indentation on his ring finger.

"Well, I spend a lot of time at the gym working out," he replied, and I thought back to the first night I'd seen him. The way the jumpsuit had fit against his body done wonders for my imagination. "I also hang out with Hector and a few other guys at the golf course. It's our responsibility to make sure the grass and landscaping stays neat and clean there."

"Oh. I didn't realize there was a golf course here on base. So you play?"

"No, I don't play. You know, all those captains and officers have to have something to do in their downtime." Jaime laughed as though it were funny, but I guessed I missed the joke.

"Do you ever go out?"

"Mostly me and my buddies just hang around and watch movies in the main room. There's a theatre on base, but we aren't allowed to go. I do get to come here whenever I want to so I try to make sure I keep a couple books on hand to read."

I honestly thought there was more to military life than what he was saying, but I'd never been around anyone who was enlisted to compare it to. I had a couple family members who were in the Army, but they didn't live close by so I rarely saw them to know what their jobs entailed. Surely, Jaime got to leave the base at some point. There was bound to be more to that job than what he'd told me because it was just not all adding up or making much sense. In fact, it actually sounded kind of boring.

He changed the subject, and we talked about music and who we both liked to listen to. I told him about the last concert I'd attended with Monica back during the summer, and Jaime shared with me that he'd never attended any kind of concert before. I felt bad for him and told him if there was one that came to this area any time soon I'd make sure he got invited since he'd truly been missing out. I still didn't like not knowing if he was married or not. Wouldn't I look stupid asking a married man to a concert that he should be attending with his wife? I struggled with how to bring up his relationship status without looking like a complete idiot.

Jaime must have noticed that sudden shift in my mood and placed his hand on my knee. I'd folded one leg underneath me when I sat so the other was planted firmly on the floor. It was a comfortable position, and now that his fingers grazed my leg, I felt immediate heat coming from his fingertips. Rather than jerk my knee away, I tried to make myself relax and enjoy the feeling of his touch.

God, please tell me he's not married. I can't have a married man putting the moves on me.

"So, Jaime, just how old are you?" I continued with another question that I felt was safe.

"How old do you think I am?" He wanted to play a guessing game with me, so I figured why not play along. If he wanted to flirt this way, I was all for it, too.

"Hmm. Let's see." I pretended to really think about it while I cocked my head to the side, giving him a flirty look. "I'd say you're probably twenty-eight or twenty-nine." While he did look to be about that age, deep inside I hoped my guess was pretty accurate. I didn't need to hear him say he was too much older than that. I'd really be pushing my limits if he was.

Jaime laughed. "You're kidding, right?" He slowly made circle patterns on my leg with his fingers, and I found myself wanting to slide over closer in hopes he might try something else. Was he a risk-taker? And if he was, how far would I allow this to go?

I felt my cheeks redden, because I was obviously way off when it came to guessing his age.

"Don't be embarrassed," he told me. "I'm thirty-two. How old are you?"

"Wow. Thirty-two. I would have never guessed." I felt like crawling underneath the couch cushions. Here I was flirting with Jaime, letting him caress my leg, and he was thirteen years older than me. Thirteen years older! Suddenly, I felt so young sitting next to him.

"Don't avoid the question now. I told you my age, so what's yours?"

"Oh. You don't really want to know."

Now, Jaime traced his fingers along the inside of my leg. I didn't want him to stop, but I also didn't want Ray to walk up and catch us flirting with each other, either.

"Let me guess. You're twenty-four."

"Not hardly. I'm nineteen." I looked down at his fingers moving over my leg, and he pulled his hand back, apparently caught off guard by my answer. "You don't have to stop," I told him.

Ray came around the corner at the same time, and it was probably a good thing Jaime had stopped. "Sorry about the interruption. I had a situation with work."

Jaime and I looked at each other, and then quickly turned away. If Ray had seen or suspected anything, he didn't let on.

Jaime looked down at his watch. "Guys, the bus is coming early tonight so I really need to be heading outside."

I hated hearing that just when I thought we'd made progress. Had my young age scared him off?

"I could take you home," I quickly offered.

Ray snickered, and I suddenly felt like an idiot, throwing myself out there.

"That's all right. I don't mind taking the bus." Jaime glared at Ray, and I pretended not to notice.

I stood and gathered my things from the table, not wanting to show the embarrassment that I felt creep up on my face. Jaime stood next to me, and I sensed his closeness. I fought back tears that had made their way into my eyes. I would not cry in front of them. Obviously, I'd made an utter fool of myself, and I was now convinced, more than ever, that Jaime was hiding something. Since he hadn't wanted me to take him home, then there had to be someone else. A wife, a girlfriend, something he didn't want me to find out.

"I'll see you all in class next week. Have a good weekend," Jaime told us, but he stared at me as spoke.

"Bye, Jaime," I said, not looking up. I didn't want to be rude, but my feelings were hurt.

"Later, man," Ray mumbled.

I was cautious with what I said with Ray, so I pretended not to be disappointed that our night was coming to an end. I really wanted Jaime to walk me out to my car so he could explain things further and so I could see him for a few more minutes, but he quickly headed to the elevator, and I heard the *ding* as the door opened. Now, walking toward the elevator, I was sad he hadn't held it for me. It closed just as I walked up. It was just as well. I mashed the button for it to go down and waited for it to come back up.

By the time the elevator reached the second floor again, Ray stood beside me, waiting to go down as well. Once the door opened, we both stepped on and didn't say a word the entire way down.

"See ya," Ray called.

"Goodnight."

I looked around, hoping to see Jaime standing at the bus stop as I walked out to my car in the parking lot, but there was no one around. He must have arrived just on time.

The entire drive home, images of Jaime with his hand on my leg filled my mind. I kept asking myself, was it possible he was seeing someone and that was the real reason he'd left so suddenly when I'd offered him a ride? It was the only thing that made sense.

I wished Monica were there so I could get her opinion. She'd be able to tell me what I needed to do.

Chapter Five

ON SATURDAY, I HAD LUNCH with my mom at one of those sandwich shops that served all kinds of healthy meats and wraps. Since the divorce, she'd distanced herself more from my sister and me. While we figured she was just dealing with the divorce in her own way, Beth and I weren't stupid. We knew she was seeing someone, which was okay, but it felt strange to know my mother was dating or had a boyfriend. Things that had never really been important before, such as her weight, hair, and makeup, were suddenly at the top of her priority list. Now, it was crucial that she ate healthy so she could be more conscious of her weight. It was no secret. I'd heard the rumors that were going around about my father seeing a younger woman, and I was pretty sure my mom had heard them, too. If my father wanted to date someone younger, it was his business, but I didn't want to hear about it right now. I had my own issues to think about when it came to age. *Like thirteen years difference.*

I'd tried calling Monica last night, because I was desperate to talk to someone, but I'd ended up leaving her a voice mail instead when she hadn't answered her phone. I even tried calling her again this morning, but she still wasn't answering.

Mom and I shared small talk while waiting on our food. She asked how school was going and seemed rather surprised when I told her how I'd been wrong about Bishop. I was actually enjoying my classes so far, and was looking forward to going back on Monday. I mentioned some of the assignments I was working on, including the group project in my world religions class. I couldn't bring myself to mention Jaime, though. Some things were just better left unsaid when it came to your mother.

The thought occurred to me that neither Jaime nor I had mentioned exchanging phone numbers. I realize it was just one more indicator that he wasn't single, but in the back of my mind, I still had that little bit of hope. There had to be a legitimate reason for his previous behavior.

I felt my face redden just thinking about it.

"Honey, are you okay?" Mom asked, taking me away from my thoughts.

"I'm fine, Mom. I just remembered something I was planning to work on this weekend."

After our lunch, I tried my best to enjoy an afternoon of shopping at the mall. Mom helped me pick out a couple new outfits, and all I could think about was wearing them in front of Jaime. Was I wrong for wanting to show off my new wraparound top that sort of revealed a little too much cleavage? I know it was more suitable for wearing out, but I kept thinking how cute it'd look with my denim skirt and ballet flats.

I also tried on a pair of heels that were to die for. They weren't classroom appropriate, but maybe I could find something to pair them with for one of the nights we met at the library. I could always say I'd come straight from work and hadn't had time to change. Only Jaime would know the truth, since none of the others knew I worked at a clothing boutique at the mall. It could be our secret.

This whole thing was getting out of control, at least on my part. My mind was going places it'd never been before.

On Sunday, I treated myself to a manicure and pedicure and decided to pay a visit to the tanning salon. Even though I'd spent time out in the sun over the summer, I wanted to add a little more color to my already sun-kissed glow. Anything to get Jaime's attention.

Later that night, I finished my essay for English class, and then looked over my notes for my religions class. I couldn't afford to get behind on anything, especially this class. According to the syllabus, we were having our first test the following week, and I made a mental note to see if Jaime wanted to meet next weekend at the library so we could prepare together.

*****

On Tuesday night, I dressed in my new wraparound top, mini skirt, and a really cute pair of sandals. I couldn't make myself wear the heels just yet. I picked out a long necklace that hung just at the top of my breasts. *I was seriously losing my mind if I thought this was going to go unnoticed*. I needed a quick reminder this wasn't some club I was going to. It was a freaking classroom. A classroom about religion at that! *Seriously, get a grip, Erica.*

I parked next to the road so I could watch for the bus to arrive. I wanted to plan it just right and walk up as soon as Jaime got off, instead of him finding me already seated in the classroom. Looking in my rearview mirror, I rechecked my hair and makeup for the third time. I'd never been so worried about my appearance. The previous guys I'd dated—you know, the ones closer to my own age—hadn't really cared how much time and effort I'd put into making myself pretty. Their main concern had been getting laid, regardless of what my hair and makeup had looked like.

Speaking of age, could I honestly date someone thirteen years older than me? I mean, it wasn't as if he *looked* that much older. I'd seen couples like that, but it was usually a much older man, like fifty or sixty, with a young twenty-something year old blonde who was just after his money and waiting for him die. I mean, what could two people so far apart in age really have in common with each other?

Jaime, on the other hand? There was some kind of attraction, and I think he felt it, too. He had, after all, made a few attempts at touching my leg and standing close behind me.

I looked down at the time on my phone and realized I needed to be heading inside to class or I was going to be late. The bus still hadn't shown up, and I wondered if maybe it'd come early and I'd just missed it.

Walking into the classroom, I looked around and noticed none of the guys who wore the Falcon Club jumpsuits were there tonight. Not Hector. And not Jaime. I remained hopeful the bus was just running late like last time.

I took my seat next to Ray, and he did a double take at my outfit. Just the way he noticed me made me feel somewhat sick to my stomach, and I wondered if I'd made a mistake in dressing that way tonight. He was probably close in age to my father, and it just made me feel gross knowing he was checking me out.

The instructor walked in, and then closed the door behind him. He got started right away on the next chapter, and I couldn't help but feel a little down that Jaime wasn't there.

I heard the door open and close, and I quickly turned around, hoping it was him. Sadly, it wasn't. Another student had come in late and sat at one of the tables in the back row. I looked over at Ray, and he shook his head. It was as if he knew. Seeing the disappointment on my face, he knew there was something going on.

After the first hour, Professor Jordon released us for a break.

"You know, you need to stop putting yourself out there for him," Ray mumbled before standing.

"Excuse me?" I knew I must have had a really strange look on my face, but I wasn't exactly sure I'd heard him correctly.

"Do you know how silly you look?" he went on to degrade me. "It's obvious you don't know much about him or his friends."

I realized Ray was trying to tell me something that I'd obviously overlooked. "I'm not sure I know what you're implying."

"For crying out loud. Do you not know what the Falcon Club is?" He said it as if I was stupid or something.

I shook my head, confused.

"They're federal inmates, Erica. You're practically throwing yourself at him, and it looks absurd. You're much better than that."

I wanted to literally crawl under the table and die. Had I just heard him correctly? Had he said federal inmates? That Jaime was in prison? I wasn't prepared for that bit of information at all.

My stomach knotted, and I did my best to keep from throwing up. How had I missed that the gray jumpsuits were for prisoners and not a military group?

Ray laughed again, and then headed out of the classroom.

Still in shock, I grabbed my purse and books and literally ran to my car. I couldn't sit in the classroom any longer, especially next to Ray, knowing the way I'd been flirting with Jaime. My God, I must be a complete moron not to have seen that. Thank goodness he wasn't there tonight to see this all take place. And what the heck was he in prison for?

The more I thought about it, the more I couldn't help myself. I opened the car door and threw up. I hadn't eaten much today, but everything came up. I coughed and tried not to choke from the bile that burned my throat.

This had to be one of the stupidest things I think I'd ever done in my life. And now, how was I going to fix it?

Instead of going home I decided to drive around to clear my head. I rolled down the car windows and let the night air fill the inside. The fresh air felt good against my clammy skin. I couldn't stay on base any longer, because it only made me think of him, so I left and headed out of town toward my former neighborhood. I passed my old high school and realized just how much I missed it. We were all so young and innocent just a couple months ago. Things had been so simple back then. Just when I was starting to really enjoy my first year of college, I had to do something stupid like flirt with a convict.

Okay, so maybe *flirt* was putting it lightly. Had my life been so distraught that I was blinded by something that was so obvious to everyone else? A federal inmate was a big deal. I smacked my forehead. It was no wonder Ray laughed when I'd offered to take Jaime home.

Later that night, when I realized the situation wasn't going to get any better, I finally decided to go home. I prayed my mom and Beth would already be in bed so I wouldn't have to explain why I was so upset.

I curled up in my bed and buried my head underneath my pillow. It wasn't the most comfortable position, since I was having a hard time breathing, but I felt as if I were hidden away from the world, away from anyone else who'd been aware of what I'd been doing. I was ashamed and deeply embarrassed. I cried to the point I no longer had any tears left. Finally, I drifted off to sleep.

Over and over I kept seeing images of Jaime with his beautiful smile, ponytail, and muscular arms. Then I'd see him standing behind bars with his arms handcuffed behind his back. None of it made sense to me. If he was in prison, then why was he free to roam around? On the other hand, what if Ray was just making it all up? It'd be a cruel joke if it was made up, but I had to get to the bottom of it.

The next morning, I awoke with a terrible headache. My eyes were red and swollen and I felt horrible. Anyone else would have thought I was coming down with something.

Mom knocked on the door and startled me. "Honey, are you awake? You're going to be late for work."

I rolled over and pretended to go back to sleep, but it didn't stop her from walking into my room to check on me. I opened my eyes to find her standing over my bed. When she saw my face, she immediately leaned over to place her hand on my forehead as though checking to see if I had a fever.

"Baby, are you coming down with something?" I detected the concerned tone in her voice, but I couldn't bring myself to tell her the truth.

Finally, I lowered the covers from my face. "I don't feel so good, Mom."

"I'll call Joann and tell her you're not coming in today. You just stay right here in bed."

I felt bad for not being honest with my mother, but I just wanted some time to myself. I needed time to think about the mess I'd gotten myself into and how I planned to handle it. I couldn't just ditch the group. After all, our grade depended on participation, and I didn't think dropping the class was the answer, either. What was I going to do?

Staying home from work today was my only option. I wasn't even sure I'd feel up to going to class tonight, either.

Mom came back into my room with a glass of juice and some Tylenol. "Here, sweetie. Take these and hopefully they'll make you feel better."

I tried to sit up so I wouldn't spill the juice all over myself, but it only made the pain in my head hurt worse.

"Thanks, Mom." Taking the medicine wouldn't hurt me since I truly wasn't ill in the way she suspected. I'd almost rather be sick with the flu than have to deal with the situation at hand.

"Joann said to tell you she hoped you felt better soon."

Mom and my boss were good friends, so I knew Joann would be sympathetic.

After I heard the front door close, and I knew my mother was gone for the day, I crawled out of bed. One look at my reflection in the bathroom mirror and I was ready to crawl back underneath the covers. I poured a cup of coffee, but couldn't bring myself to drink it. My nerves were shot and my stomach couldn't handle anything right now.

After grabbing my pillow and my favorite blanket, I curled up on the couch, and it wasn't long before I fell into a deep sleep.

*****

The sound of my phone ringing woke me up. I knew from the ringtone it was my mother, probably calling to check on me, but I let her leave a voicemail and rolled over onto my back.

I stared up at the ceiling, trying to figure out how I was going to deal with all of this. I mean, I couldn't totally blame Jaime for me being clueless. How was he supposed to know I had no idea what the Falcon Club meant? I was sure he thought I'd been playing right along. Come to think of it, when I'd mentioned taking him home that night, he'd reacted strangely. So there I was, thinking he'd turned me down because he was married. Ha! I'd almost rather have found out he was married than to find out all of this.

My mind was flooded with a million questions.

Weren't inmates supposed to wear striped outfits with plastic shoes? Wait a minute. If Jaime was in prison, why was he, as well as the other guys in my classes, allowed to attend college and mingle with everyone else? Shouldn't he be locked up behind bars with tight security? Was he a possible threat?

I realized it wasn't doing me any good to lay there. I took a long, hot shower and was disappointed I'd wasted the majority of the day. My class tonight wasn't out on the military base, but rather at the main campus. However, I was supposed to be meeting Jaime, Hector, and Ray shortly afterward at the library so we could work on our project again. I wondered if I could bring myself to make it. Could I look at Jaime or Ray the same anymore? Or could I put up a front and pretend it didn't bother me?

I bet Ray was still laughing about the look on my face last night when he'd made his announcement. He was a jerk and I didn't like him one bit.

Chapter Six

I WALKED INTO MY ENGLISH class behind a couple other students. Up on the dry erase board was a note from the instructor.

Class cancelled tonight. Please see syllabus for class assignment and take one of the handouts from the front table. Class will resume next week.

That was just great! What was I supposed to do while I waited until it was time to go to the library? Had I known class would be cancelled, I probably would have just stayed at home and said screw the library, but I'd forced myself to get ready. I had to face the truth eventually.

I'd made up my mind that I wasn't going to let this drag me down any more than what it already had. Ray may have made me out to be a joke, but I'd show him. He may have seen me as weak and naïve, but I wasn't going to let him have the last laugh.

I grabbed an iced coffee at the campus coffee shop downstairs, and then sipped on it as I drove out to the military base. It was the only thing I'd had all day and I hoped it wouldn't make me sick to my stomach. I figured I might as well take advantage of some study time before the guys showed up.

The entire drive, my hands trembled, and I found it hard to hold on to my cup. And to make matters worse, as I handed over my military pass to the guard manning the entrance, I accidentally dropped it and he had to step outside the gatehouse to pick it up. *Get a grip, Erica. Stay focused and strong.* I kept telling myself that over and over.

"Have a good evening, ma'am." He saluted me and waved me on through.

I parked as close to the library as I could, and then looked around the parking lot before getting out of my car. There was no sign of anyone, and I hoped I could sneak inside without being noticed. I tossed my bag over my shoulder and walked as quickly as I could.

Our usual meeting spot was on the second floor, so I went up to grab a table. Hopefully, there'd be an available one facing the elevators so I could keep an eye on who got there first. I didn't want any surprises tonight.

As I stepped out of the elevator, I noticed it was quieter than normal. I placed my bag onto the table, and then went to the bathroom. I took my time, double checking my appearance before I walked back out. I hoped no one noticed the puffiness that was still underneath my eyes. I'd definitely toned down my clothes this evening, too, opting for a t-shirt and khaki shorts. And they weren't short-short, either! In fact, they looked more like the shorts that we were allowed to wear in high school. My knees were barely visible underneath the hem, if that tells you anything. I was definitely going for the "scaled back" look so no one got the wrong impression about me tonight. *That's right, Ray. Kiss my ass! Let's see what you think of* this *outfit.*

I grabbed a sip of water from the water fountain and swished it around in my mouth to get rid of the coffee I still tasted. Once I turned around to walk back to the table, I thought I was going to choke before I could finish swallowing. I coughed uncontrollably, embarrassed once again.

Sitting on the couch across from the table, where I'd left my bag, was Jaime. This was a different Jaime from what I'd seen just last week. He still wore his gray jumpsuit, but his hair had been cut. And when I say cut, it was more than just a trim. His ponytail was gone and it was almost as short as a crewcut style. I did a double take and my insides tightened.

"Hello." Just hearing his voice and his accent sent goose bumps throughout my body.

"Hhh… Hi yourself. Wh…What are you doing here already?" I stuttered my words, making it obvious that he'd taken me by surprise. It didn't matter how badly I wanted to be mad at him because of the situation, I just couldn't. Technically, he hadn't done anything wrong.

"I wanted to see you." He patted the seat next to him on the couch.

"But how did you know I'd get here early?" *Heck, even I hadn't known that.*

"I didn't." His eyes were a beautiful golden-brown tonight, almost like creamy milk chocolate. They were drawing me to him.

"Then how did you know I was already here and this was my stuff?"

I should have been nervous, especially since finding out Jaime was a convict, but nothing about this conversation frightened me in the least. My body told me to take a seat next to him. I was doing everything within my power to stand still and not join him just yet, but the forces pulled me to him.

What would anyone else think if they walked up and saw us seated so close together? A convict and a civilian. I was convinced I was the only one who hadn't known what that gray jumpsuit symbolized.

"Erica?"

The sound of Jaime suddenly calling my name brought me back to the present.

"Sorry. I was just thinking about something."

"Obviously."

"So, how did you know I was here?" I asked again, since I didn't know if he'd already answered my previous question while I'd been lost in my thoughts.

"I watched you." His accent tonight was more prevalent than it'd ever been before.

"You watched me?"

"Yes, from the window back there. I stood there staring outside when I saw your car pull in."

"You didn't know I was going to get here early."

"And you didn't know I'd be here early, either."

Jaime gave me a once over, and I suddenly felt like a school girl. Looking down at the floor, I couldn't believe I'd walked out of my house dressed like this. He stood and walked over to me since I still hadn't taken a seat yet. Using his finger, he lifted my chin so I looked at him.

I was captured under his spell. I was mesmerized.

"Is something wrong?" he asked, noticing my behavior. "And what's up with this?" He pointed down at my clothes.

"I just thought maybe the clothes I'd been wearing were a little too revealing." I cringed as I said that.

"Say what? According to whom? I was actually enjoying the little show you were giving me each night." And what would he have thought last night had he seen my low-cut wraparound top? Ray had surely noticed.

"Show? What show?" For the first time I felt uneasy and pretended to be dumb.

"Come on, Erica. You know you were dressing like that just to turn me on."

"I was?" I bit my tongue, suddenly wishing I could take back those words.

Jaime laughed. "You're such a tease."

"No, I'm not." I lightly pushed at his chest and realized the uneasiness was suddenly gone. I was back to flirting with him once again.

Jaime reached up and grabbed my hand. Holding it for a few seconds, he continued. "You know you drive me crazy."

If I could scream right now, I would. I would scream as loudly as I could until I woke up from this dream. Wait. I'm not having a dream. This was really happening.

"Jaime, I... I need to ask..."

"Come on, grab your things and let's get away from this front area. There's a quieter place in the back."

Quiet? There was no one else around and he was worried about it being quiet. I, on the other hand, was worried about Hector or Ray walking up and catching us carrying on like this.

Not resisting him at all, I followed him around the corner, walking past rows and rows of bookshelves. There were several computer stations set up, but no one was using them tonight. It was apparent we were the only ones on this floor.

All the way in the very back, I noticed another clearing between the rows of shelves with several more tables set up, only there were no computers there. Two more couches sat across from one another, their leather more worn than the couch I'd previously sat on. One thing was certain: This library was massive. I'd almost be willing to bet that hardly anyone frequented this part of it. Who knew what could happen up there? And that was what concerned me. What *could* happen?

I noticed a row of windows off to the side.

"Is that where you watched me?" I asked, pointing to the windows.

Jaime stepped closer, so close I felt the heat coming from his body.

"You don't like me watching you?" He reached up and lightly ran his finger down the side of my cheek, and I took a step toward him.

"Uh, of course I don't mind."

Jaime twisted a piece of my hair that had fallen loose from the clip around his finger.

"Aren't you afraid someone will see us together? Isn't that against the rules or something?" There, I'd finally said something that pertained to him being in prison. I had to wonder if I was foolish for allowing this to come this far.

"Hardly anyone comes back here. And even if they did, we're working on a project, right?" If he'd picked up on my subtle hint, he didn't show it.

I knew that was what we were supposed to be doing, but we were far from working on any assignment. The least we should do is pull out our books or something to make it appear as if we were working.

"Aren't there cameras? What if they're watching us?" I continued to interrogate him.

"Dang it, Erica. What's with all the questions?" His tone shifted, and I could tell he was getting frustrated.

All of my questions had clearly killed the moment.

Or so I thought.

"I just… Ray said…"

And before I could say more, he leaned over and kissed me gently on the lips. His were soft and moist. I was uncertain how to respond.

I stopped from leaning more into him and pulled back. If I'd struggled to get my words out before, I was absolutely speechless now. Jaime kept looking at my lips as if he wanted to kiss them again. I caught myself running my tongue over them to dampen them. And yes, I wanted him to kiss me again, too. It was interesting, to say the least.

"Jaime, we can't. Someone might see us." I did it anyway. I leaned forward and he responded by bringing his lips to mine.

This time I heard a slight moan coming from him. He, too, was enjoying this moment.

"Mmm. Your lips are so soft," he whispered. "I've dreamed about kissing them since the first night of class."

I nearly melted onto the floor just hearing him say that.

A few rows over, someone cleared their throat. Startled, we both jumped and separated quickly. We thought we'd been up there alone. Not sure if the other person saw us or was just in the area, but we needed to be careful. And speaking of being careful, I was suddenly reminded of Ray.

"Um, Jaime. Can I ask you something?" There was no easy way to broach this subject other than being straight forward. Please, just let Ray be making this up, I kept saying to myself as I gathered in my mind the right words to say. I took a seat on the couch.

"Sure, babe. What's up?"

Why did he have to call me babe? Now, of all times. It was as if we'd reached a different level of understanding with each other just because of a simple kiss. A simple kiss, not hardly. It wasn't making it any easier, that was for sure. Here went nothing.

"In class the other day, Ray told me something that I've been having a hard time believing." So far, I was off to a good start.

"Oh yeah? What's that?" Jaime had no idea what I was about to ask him. He sounded so casual.

"With this being my first semester at Bishop and my first time ever being on a military base, I guess I didn't realize there would be other students also taking classes with me."

"Okay. I'm not following you." He kept his attention focused on me, obviously confused with where I was going.

I hated to be blunt, but he left me no other choice. So I spit it out.

"Ray said the reason you wear that jumpsuit is because you're, uh, in prison here." I said it quickly, hoping I wouldn't have to repeat myself. "Did I miss something somewhere, because I thought being locked up meant you were behind bars? Please tell me this is just a sick joke Ray is playing on me." Tears pooled in my eyes, but I refused to cry. I would not cry about this in front of him. I may be embarrassed, but I couldn't deny the feelings that I'd started having for him before Ray made his announcement.

Jaime reached up and rubbed his forehead. "You mean to tell me you didn't know about this ridiculous outfit? The Falcon Club?" Jaime reached down and tugged at the front of the jumpsuit.

I shook my head and let out a deep sigh. "No, I didn't. Is Ray right?" I suddenly felt terrible for asking.

"Look, Erika. I thought you knew. God, I thought you knew." From the shock that was evident on his face, I could tell it bothered him.

"Jaime, am I going to get in trouble for being here with you? I mean, if this isn't right…"

Just a few minutes ago, we'd been kissing and discovering the possibility of something more, but now, there we were, facing the bitter truth.

Jaime reached up to run his fingers through his hair, as if forgetting it'd all been cut off.

"We just have to be careful."

"You can't be serious. Careful? So we *aren't* supposed to be here together?"

I tensed when I realized just how much trouble I could get into. I mean, it wasn't as if anything had really happened, but I sat alone with a convicted felon. What in the hell had I gotten myself into?

"It's not like that at all. Just listen to me. Okay?" he pleaded.

Jaime explained everything, and I forgot all about meeting up with Hector and Ray. I listened intently to every word he said. Technically, the inmates weren't supposed to have any contact with the other students, but because they were working on group assignments, such as our situation, we were allowed to work together only in the classroom and library. Inmates were to remain visible to the instructors at all times and must remain in clear view of military personnel when not in the classroom. Students and civilians weren't to engage in private conversations with the federal prisoners, and at no time was it acceptable for inmates to borrow or use personal property belonging to students. This included anything from school supplies to cell phones. It was the inmate's responsibility to provide their own necessary items for class.

I was having a hard time with everything he'd told me and I was sure the expression on my face said as much. This was some serious shit.

"I'm really sorry you had to find out this way," he apologized. "Before you get upset or scared, prison here is a lot different than what you're thinking."

Truth be known, I honestly didn't know what I was thinking at that point.

"None of the guys here are bad or out to harm you, so you can relax. They're not murderers or rapists. They're here for drug trafficking, tax evasion, or embezzlement. Things like that. Yes, the crimes are still serious, but it's not like they killed anyone or they're on death row."

"What did you do to end up here?" I couldn't believe I asked him to confess his crime. Was it any of my business?

As painful as it had to be for him, he continued. "It all started about eleven years ago. I was hanging with the wrong person somewhere I shouldn't have been. You see, my mom worked hard raising our family, and no matter how much I tried to work and help out, it just wasn't enough. We were always coming up short. Good jobs were hard to come by, and even being bilingual didn't help. Everyone in Miami speaks two languages, and I just sort of blended in with everyone else. I had done some work before for this particular guy, Javier, and since he'd paid me good money, I decided to do some more for him again. Only this time it was a setup and I got caught.

"I got stopped by the border patrol and busted for having illegal drugs in my possession. My friend, who'd arranged the deal, ran, not wanting to get caught, and I took the fall. At first, I was locked up in one of the many jails in Miami, and let me tell you, you want to talk about rough. That place was a nightmare! My momma would come to see me during visiting hours on Sunday and all she could do was cry. It wasn't a place to bring young children, even though I watched wives bring their kids to visit with men all the time. Mom was so sad that I'd done something so stupid. All because I wanted to help our family out."

I listened intently to every word. I sensed just how painful this was for him.

"My court date was coming up, and I admit, I was nervous. Nervous as hell because this was it. My future was at stake. I didn't know what kind of sentencing the judge had in store for me, but I knew this was a serious matter. My court-appointed attorney was doing his best to plea bargain, but the district attorney showed no mercy. Drugs are a major problem in southern Florida and the state does everything they can to put a stop to it. In the end, the judge gave me ten years in the federal penitentiary. I guess maybe I was lucky. I don't know, but it could have been more."

"You've been here for ten years?" I was shocked beyond belief.

"No, the first prison I was in had tighter security. I had to do different things just to earn certain privileges. Eventually, because I'd been following the guidelines and maintaining a good track record, I had the option to transfer to another facility with the chance to take some college courses and an opportunity to work. That's how I ended up here. I haven't seen anyone in my family for nearly six years now."

"Six years? Wow, that's a really long time. Can you talk to them on the phone? Or write to them?"

"Before I came here I did get to visit with my mom one last time. She was still very bitter with the system. And she's right. There are more serious crimes being committed every day, but I happened to be the one who got caught. I didn't even do the stuff, I just delivered it. It was easy money and the deals were quick. I could make several hundred dollars just by working a few hours. It was money my family needed to survive. Believe me, I've paid my price." He paused, as if he was thinking about everything he'd just shared with me. "On the brighter side of things, I've gotten the chance to attend college. The government took up the tab the first year, but after that, it became our family's responsibility to pay for it. That's one of the reasons it's taken me six years just to complete a degree program."

"So your mom is having to pay for it now?"

I could tell this was a tender subject with Jaime when he looked away. I was pretty sure I may have even seen a tear in the corner of his eye, but he quickly wiped it away.

"She contacted my grandfather back in Columbia and they worked out some kind of deal. All I know is the money was transferred into my account, and she told me not to worry about it. How could I not worry? I mean, my mom is the only one working in the family and she works ten-hour shifts just to provide. Can you imagine six people living in a two-bedroom apartment? If it weren't for my younger brothers and sisters looking out for one another and being great kids, I'm not sure my family would be making it right now."

"But look at you now. You're getting ready to graduate, and then you'll soon be getting released. How does it feel knowing you've accomplished that?" I wanted to be positive for him.

"You don't get it, do you?" He blurted out.

"Excuse me? I don't get what?"

Jaime had quickly changed his tone, and I didn't understand what had caused the sudden mood swing.

"Can't you see how hard this has been for me? Not only have I been an embarrassment to my family, I've not exactly been a great role model for my brothers or sisters. Every day I wonder if they'll even recognize me once I'm released. My mom refused to let them see me while I was locked up in Miami. She made up some kind of story to tell them about me and that's the way it's been ever since. They think I'm off doing something good for our family. They know I'm on a military base since they see my address on the letters I send home, and probably just assume I'm a soldier and not a convicted felon."

"Jaime, I'm sorry." I reached up to rest my hand on his shoulder. Our conversation tonight had obviously been more than what either of us had anticipated. He pulled away, and suddenly I felt all alone. I had to wonder if I'd done the right thing by bringing it up, but I'd needed to know. I'd needed to know what that jumpsuit stood for.

I couldn't have gone another day without knowing the truth.

Chapter Seven

I AWOKE THE NEXT MORNING feeling totally different about Jaime. Yes, I did feel sorry for him, but I knew that wasn't what he'd want me to feel. He'd had enough sorrow the past ten years, and had plenty of time to think about his wrongdoings. He and his family had been through hell, literally, but life still went on, and he'd apparently made the most of what he could with the situation. I had to believe in my heart that he was sincere with me and not just using me. I believed he told me the truth.

In my mind, I replayed everything over and over again. Jaime and I had shared a passionate kiss, and I wondered just how far things would have progressed had I not stopped him. We'd been in a library, but with no one else around, what kind of risk would we have taken?

Then I wondered if there had been other girls. Did he meet someone new each semester? Was I just a play toy for him? Oh, why had this suddenly crossed my mind?

I struggled to make it through the day at work. I felt fine, but I was anxious to see Jaime again. I needed to know more and now. I needed to know if I was the only one. He was interesting, and I was determined to see where this led.

I spent my lunch break working on homework, and before long it was time to get off for the day. I was thankful it'd passed quickly, although I wasn't looking forward to seeing Ray and having to explain to him why we hadn't met last night. Apparently, Jaime and I had remained hidden enough Ray hadn't discovered our hiding spot. For all Ray knew, none of us had showed up. Come to think of it, neither had Hector.

When I got into line to drive through the gate on base, I noticed it seemed to take a little longer than usual for the cars to advance. In fact, the guy manning the guard station walked around each car, peering inside. I found it peculiar, but then again, I wasn't used to proper military procedure, either. For all I knew, this was something they did randomly.

Once it was my turn to pull forward, I stopped and allowed the guard to view inside my car just as he'd done the others. If that had been done from the beginning, I don't think it would have seemed odd, but my gut told me something wasn't right. Still, I felt relatively safe being on base, even now knowing there was a prison there, and quickly forgot about it once I pulled into the parking lot and found a place to park.

There seemed to be more students than normal mingling outside, and I soon learned it was because the main door leading inside the building was locked. Students formed a line as the time drew near for class to start, and I noticed everyone pulling out their IDs prior to going inside, something the guards had gotten slack on doing.

I heard the sound of the bus as it pulled up, and then the guys stepped out one by one. It didn't take long for me to spot Jaime, and he took his place at the end of the line along with the other guys from the Falcon Club.

I considered joining him but, thinking back to what I'd just recently learned, changed my mind. If he saw me, he didn't make any kind of acknowledgement, and I hoped nothing had changed since our conversation the previous night. Even if nothing else ever happened, I still considered him a friend.

Now that I knew what the Falcon Club was, I viewed each guy in a totally different way. Each of them had their own reasons for being there and they all had a story to tell. Yes, it all made sense now. Some of them looked rough on the surface where others just looked normal. The only thing separating them from the outside world was the drab gray jumpsuits they wore. They could have been dressed just like the other guys in my class with their sharp, crisp military uniforms, but regardless of what they wore on the outside, everyone had their own secrets. Even those in the military.

I finally made it through the entrance and went into the classroom. Ray was already seated and looked up when I placed my things on top the table.

"Evening, Ray," I told him, being cordial even though I despised him.

"What happened to you last night? I showed up at the library and waited. You know our grade is dependent on participation in *and* outside the classroom." He placed emphasis on outside the classroom, but Ray was an asshole, and I wasn't going to let him bother me. Not now. "I can overlook *the other two*, but what was your excuse?"

"Oh, Ray, I'm so sorry. I was sick yesterday and didn't even make it in to work. I hate that the other guys didn't show up. Maybe they just forgot we'd planned to meet." I was killing him with kindness. I hated lying and did everything I could to keep my face from showing differently. I'd had enough on my plate to think about without having to deal with him, too.

"Oh, they knew all right. Sneaky pieces of shit." Ray held nothing back. "I think one of our group members may be involved in something and got caught. Maybe that's the reason they didn't show up. I knew having a group assignment with them was a mistake."

I was doing everything in my power to keep from slapping Ray. He might not have respect for Jaime and Hector, or the others in the Falcon Club, for that matter, but there was no reason to start name calling. We were in a group for an assignment, and whether we liked it or not, we had a grade to earn. Calling them pieces of shit was completely uncalled for.

Suddenly, I froze. What was he talking about someone being involved in something? Jaime? Hector? Had someone seen Jaime and I together that night? Oh, for crying out loud! Please say it wasn't so. I wanted to run from the classroom and pretend none of last night had happened. Well, that is, the kiss we'd shared.

Jaime finally walked inside, and then took his seat beside me. Nervously, I looked over at him and tried to smile. He nodded and looked back down at his book. He was acting strange, and it concerned me, especially since hearing what Ray had said.

Professor Jordon started his lecture, and I found myself struggling to follow along. Leaning up so Ray wouldn't be able to see, I jotted down on my notepad, *U okay?* and lifted it so Jaime could read.

He printed a simple "Y," and I took it to mean "yes." He printed *U?* and I slightly nodded, not wanting to call attention to our method of communicating.

Where's Hector? I wrote next. I made sure to blacken out the words after he'd read them so no one else would see or read them.

Gone, he printed on his paper.

I was sure all the color must have left my face upon reading that one word. Gone. Not sure what he meant by gone, but I couldn't wait for our break so I could find out what the heck was going on. I tried to focus on taking notes again, but felt defeated. No matter how hard I tried to concentrate, I just couldn't. It all made sense now that Ray's remarks had been aimed at Hector and not at Jaime.

Just as soon as the instructor announced it was time for a break, I turned to look at Jaime. "What do you mean he's gone?" I couldn't get my words out quick enough.

"Hector got transferred to another location today. He and a few others got caught bringing drugs back into our facility and the warden busted them." Jaime looked around to see if anyone was watching us.

"You've got to be kidding me. Hector?" I was shocked.

"Security's been tightened up, but it will only be for a little while. It happens every semester—someone gets careless and caught. It's required to have full body searches prior to returning back to the camp now after we've been in contact with anyone outside our group. Hector and the other guys won't tell who supplied them, but the wardens are fairly certain it was coming from someone here on campus."

"You mean a student was giving it to them?" I tried to figure out how it could have happened.

Jaime kind of snickered. "Maybe. Or maybe a teacher. You never know."

"Surely a teacher wouldn't have done something like that. Right?"

"Look, Erica. For the most part, the instructors here are great and don't have a problem with us taking classes, but there are a few who don't feel it's right. Even though we pay our own way to attend, they just don't feel that inmates should be getting an education, regardless of who pays for it. They're getting paid to teach, no matter who the students are, and that's the way it should be."

I could see his point, but wouldn't a teacher be taking a huge risk by supplying drugs?

"Poor Hector."

"Well, it's not the first time I've seen this go down. Like I said, it happens almost every semester. My guys make friends, they get too comfortable, and eventually drugs come into play. It happens, so don't get all worked up over it."

"If it happens every semester, won't they start putting tighter restrictions on everything? What if they stop letting you go to class?"

"Think about it, Erica. These are government people watching over us. They don't care if we're here or in another facility somewhere else. Just like they don't care if we get sent off. The longer we stay incarcerated, the better their job security is."

It saddened me hearing that. While these guys may be doing time, it wasn't as if they murdered or raped anyone. I mean, tax evasion and drug trafficking wasn't right, either, and shouldn't lessen the punishment for the crime, but they shouldn't be treated as if they were hardcore criminals.

I sensed there was more to the story, and I noticed Jaime looking around again to see if anyone was in earshot of hearing us. Then he filled me in on the rest of the news about Hector.

Apparently, Hector had a girlfriend, someone he'd met from a previous class, and she lived close by. He didn't say if she was the one who'd been supplying the drugs for him, but I was pretty sure if it wasn't her, it was someone else involved in their circle. Hector was known for meeting her in the parking lot behind the building. She'd slip him a change of clothes, and he'd leave the base with her. Most of the time he'd duck down in the backseat or ride in the trunk, but one time he'd been so bold he rode in the front seat with her. The guard had never suspected a thing. And since they worked on rotating shifts, she would return him back to the base before class was over and their little secret remained safe once again. No one would risk telling on them. It just wasn't something you did to a fellow cellmate.

I might not think logically about everything, but I could use my imagination and pretty much figure out what they were doing when they left the base. I just couldn't imagine taking such a risk. God, were they crazy? Guys have sexual needs, and being locked up for so many years can surely make you do some stupid things, but to leave the base? It just didn't seem worth the gamble.

It got me to thinking about Jaime and what, if anything, I'd risk to see him. I didn't think I could ever do what Hector and his girlfriend did, but was my meeting him at the library putting myself in harm's way and throwing red flags in my direction? We were, after all, just friends who'd met in class.

Nothing more.

Right? I admit, the kiss had stirred emotions in me I hadn't realized were there, but looking at the facts, was this even something realistic for me and him?

*****

Once Ray came back inside the classroom, Professor Jordon called the three of us to his desk. I assumed this had to do with what Jaime had just shared with me about Hector, so I pretended not to know anything.

Without going into details, our group had obviously been reduced from four to three. Our overall grade wouldn't be counted off from Hector's non-participation, but we were expected to step up and cover the part of the assignment that he'd been responsible for.

"We'll get right on it, sir," Jaime quickly added, trying to make this transition smooth for us all. It was bad enough Hector had put us in this predicament, but there was no need to dwell on it. We had another month before the assignment was due, and there was plenty of time to overcome the loss of Hector.

"I bet you will. Right on it," Ray said with a slight sneer to his voice as he looked at me.

Jaime and I both cut our gazes in Ray's direction, neither of us appreciating his tone.

After taking our seats again, class resumed, and I couldn't wait for it to be over. Too much had happened in the last twenty-four hours, and I was having trouble letting it all sink in. There was no reason for me to turn against Jaime, and neither should Ray. We would somehow make it through this project.

The next evening, Jaime suggested taking a break from meeting up at the library. He said everything would settle down in a couple days and right now, he didn't want anyone reading more into our meetings. The last thing he wanted was for me to feel uncomfortable. Ray was just being an ass like always and I shouldn't worry.

The rest of the week seemed to drag. I missed seeing Jaime and wondered if he missed me, too.

Chapter Eight

ON FRIDAY MORNING I PACKED my things and got ready to make the five-hour drive to spend the weekend with Monica. I should have been thrilled to see my best friend, but I couldn't keep my mind from thinking about Jaime. I was saddened he hadn't wanted to meet up last night, even though I understood his reasoning since the ordeal that had happened with Hector. Things did need to settle down.

Hopefully, my mood would change once I arrived on campus. It was homecoming for State, and Monica had plans for us to hang out tonight on the Square for the parade followed by the pep rally. Then tomorrow, she had tickets for us to attend the game.

Monica had someone she wanted me to meet, and I found myself dreading this more than anything. According to her, he was totally "hot and irresistible." She was convinced I'd be eager to transfer next semester and would figure out some way to cover the expenses. What she wasn't aware of was that my opinion of Bishop had changed recently and that I was actually enjoying it now.

Of course *certain individuals* may have swayed those feelings, but it was, honestly, not as bad as I'd originally thought.

For most of the drive, I thought about Jaime and the story he'd shared with me about his family. I couldn't imagine being away from my own, even if they were divorced for ten years. And while the age factor had been a big deal for me at one point, it wasn't so much anymore now that we'd gotten to know each other a little better. I thought about the other friends I had who were older than me, like my boss, Joann, or the even the parents of my friends. Sure, they were older, but age was really only a number. It was more about how you acted and carried yourself.

Right now, though, Jaime and I were merely friends and nothing more. That's right, we were *just* friends. There was no reason to read more into the situation than what was really there. Okay, so we'd shared a kiss. Big deal. It wasn't as if we were in a relationship, which couldn't happen anyway since he was in prison. Right? I really hoped I could talk about all of it with Monica this weekend and get her opinion. I didn't need her passing any judgement when I told her I wasn't really interested in being fixed up with anyone right now. I could hear her now. She'd tell me I was insane and wrong about this thing with Jaime, especially when I'd tell her the part about him being incarcerated. I decided to just feel her out before mentioning specific details. As my best friend, she shouldn't judge me, but I know how my first reaction would be if she was to tell me a similar story.

I pulled into the parking lot of her apartment and remembered the first time she and I had come there to visit. We were high school seniors anxious to take the next big step in our lives. Two best friends living the good life—our own apartment, partying, you name it, we were going to do it. Just went to show how quickly things could change in the blink of an eye. Thanks Mom and Dad, I owe you one!

Before I was able to send a text to Monica to let her know I was there, I looked up to see her running down the steps toward my car.

I jumped out and I gave my best friend a hug. I'd missed her terribly.

"Let me look at you. It feels like forever since we've seen each other." She squealed as she took my hand and spun me around before giving me another gigantic hug. It hadn't been *that* long, but it was still good to see her.

"Help me grab my things. I hope you've got something to eat, because I'm starving," I told her.

Even though I was only staying for two nights, I somehow managed to pack two suitcases that were loaded down with clothes and shoes. I wasn't certain what I should wear being on a "real" college campus, so I'd brought along several outfits. Monica would help me decide so I'd blend right in with everyone.

"We're meeting up with some of my friends over at Wings n' Things, so as soon as you're ready, we'll go on over. They can't wait to meet you." I knew she was looking forward to introducing me to her new circle, but I honestly just wanted to spend a quiet evening with her, maybe get a pizza, and have some serious girl talk.

Neither of us was old enough to drink, but we'd spent many nights sipping Kool-Aid in our *Best Friends* wineglasses while we'd chatted about the boys in our lives. Those were the days.

Quite frankly, neither of us had seriously dated much—we'd preferred each other's company over that of some silly high school boy—but now that we'd reached adulthood, I yearned for our conversations to go to the next level. I needed some honesty about what was going on with my life, but I somehow didn't feel Monica would be so understanding of Jaime. She didn't sense anything was wrong, though, so I decided to hold off on bringing anything up just yet. I'd just have to save it for later.

Since I hadn't been able to share the apartment with her, she'd been left to find a roommate on her own. I felt terrible about it all, but it hadn't taken her long to find someone to replace me. In fact, she'd actually gotten pretty lucky. Mandy, the new roommate, spent the majority of her time over at her boyfriend's place, so Monica, for the most part, had the apartment all to herself. Mandy still paid her half of the expenses, and Monica was cool with that. I'd be staying in Mandy's room for the weekend and was glad, since I'd never been one for sleeping on the couch.

I quickly changed into jeans and a sweater and pulled my hair up in a ponytail. I have a bad habit of twisting my hair while I drive or when I'm pre-occupied. In this case, I'd had a double dose, so my hair looked a bit flat. A ponytail was a great alternative when having a bad hair day.

Monica drove for us since she pretty much had learned her way around campus now. The college atmosphere there was definitely different from what I'd experienced at Bishop. We arrived at Wings 'n Things, and then headed to a back table. There were already six other people seated, as well as three empty chairs.

Monica made the introductions, and everyone seemed nice and friendly—a group I could have blended well with, too. I sat next to a guy named Greg, and figured this was the guy Monica was so anxious for me to meet. He looked harmless enough and was sort of cute, but I just wasn't feeling up for matchmaking.

I listened to everyone talk about what was going on in their lives and I couldn't help but notice how juvenile they were all sounding. God, I was being such a bitch to think that about them. I needed to stop this mess right now. Just because they were enjoying themselves and living in a completely different environment, it didn't give me the right to put them down because they were having a good time. I was sure if I'd been there from the beginning of the semester, I'd be laughing right along with them and it wouldn't seem so juvenile then.

I nibbled on some chips and salsa that was in the center of the table, and then sipped on my Coke. Everyone was hyped up about the game, and they should be. After all, this was what college life was all about and what I'd yearned for at one time.

Finally, we placed our meal orders with a guy named Dave, and Monica flirted shamelessly with him. After he walked away, she filled me in on the couple dates they'd been on, and I completely understood her behavior. Dave and Greg were roommates and that was why she'd wanted us to meet. Both guys were attending the game with us tomorrow, and she hoped I didn't mind her already making the arrangements.

Dave was cute and totally Monica's type. He was tall with dark blond hair that hung down into his eyes. I picked up on the way he'd toss his head to the side, causing his bangs to fall back in place. He looked preppy and fit the rich boy mold to a T. It made me question what my type was. Up until now, I probably would have found Dave attractive, too, but something inside had changed.

Not wanting to seem rude, Greg and I talked, and I found myself enjoying the conversation. Monica was right. He was really sweet once I got to know him.

After an hour or so, we each took care of our own meal tickets, and then everyone headed outside. I heard the band playing in the distance along with the sounds of cheers and chants. The parade was underway and the streets were getting crowded.

"Come on, the parade is starting." Monica grabbed hold of my hand and pulled me up to the curb. Greg followed behind, as well as the others in our group, and we claimed our spots just outside Wings 'n Things.

Before long, the parade procession was directly in front of us and it was hard not to feel the same excitement as everyone else. I joined in the cheering and chanting as each float passed. Greg stepped closer behind me, and when he wasn't waving his hands, trying to catch the mini footballs and other knickknacks the parade revelers threw out, he'd place his hand on the small of my back.

At first, I wanted to pull away, but I realized he wasn't doing any harm. If he read more into it, then it was completely on him, because I wasn't sending him mixed signals.

Finally, when all of the football players, cheerleaders, and the band had gone by, the noise level went down so we weren't yelling at each other just to hear what the other had to say. Greg grabbed hold of my hand, and I followed him and Monica to the restaurant again. Dave's shift was ending, and we were all going to ride to her apartment together.

While waiting for Dave, Monica and I went to the bathroom and it didn't take long for her to start asking questions.

"So, what do you think about Dave? He's so perfect for me, don't you think? And what about Greg? Do you like him so far? Doesn't he have the most gorgeous eyes?"

I flushed the toilet and was spared a few seconds to think about everything she asked. As I walked up to the sink to wash my hands, Monica was fixing her hair. She stared at my reflection in the mirror, barely able to control her giddiness.

"Well?" She couldn't wait for my response.

"Well, what?" I pretended not to know what she was asking about.

"Come on, Erica. What do you think? Dave? Greg? Tell me."

"You and Dave look good together. Are you guys serious?" I wanted to play it safe and steer away from any questions related to Greg.

"Yes, we're exclusively a couple, if that's what you're asking." From the look on her face it was evident they'd already "done" something to secure their relationship. It made me wonder if anyone ever waited to have sex anymore. Was there any value in waiting for the right person to come along? Or was it something we felt was necessary to do to secure our relationships?

I opened the bathroom door and walked out, thankful I'd avoided having to comment on Greg. The guys sat just outside the door, waiting for us.

As we crawled into Monica's car to leave, she handed over the keys to Dave while Greg and I took the backseat. I interacted with their conversations the best I could, but I found myself staring out the window, looking up at the sky. I wondered what Jaime was doing tonight and if he, too, was looking at the stars. What was it like being in prison?

"Erica?" I was brought out of my trance by the sound of Monica's voice.

"I'm sorry, what?"

"Just wondering if you were up for a movie tonight. We could stop and pick up something at the Redbox if you aren't too tired."

I pretended to yawn and almost immediately felt bad for doing it. I was tired, but the truth was, I wanted to be alone with Monica.

"Maybe tomorrow night?" I suggested. "I'm pretty exhausted from the long drive."

Greg reached for my hand again, and I prayed it wasn't much farther to drop off the guys. He rubbed his thumb over the top of my hand, and instead of it having a desirable effect on me, I found myself silently praying he'd just stop. Under any other circumstances, I'd have been all for this, but I just wasn't feeling it.

Not tonight.

Probably never.

I just didn't want to hurt Monica's feelings. I knew she meant well, but there was so much I needed to tell her.

After we dropped the guys off at their apartment, I climbed into the front while Monica slid over to the driver's seat. She gave Dave a kiss goodbye, and thank goodness, Greg just sort of waved at me.

We were silent the rest of the way to her apartment. Maybe she thought I'd fallen asleep or something, because she hadn't said anything, either. Once we got inside, I called dibs on the bathroom first.

I washed off my makeup and then rinsed out the washcloth so it wouldn't stain—something that always annoyed my mom. I looked up in the mirror and laughed at my raccoon eyes. I loved wearing heavy coats of mascara on my long lashes, but sometimes it was a bitch to remove. I disliked the oily feeling left on my skin by using those removers, so I stuck with using my favorite cold cream. Mom had recommended it years ago, and I'd used it ever since.

"Still using that cream stuff, huh?" Monica laughed as I poured myself a glass of water. She sat at the table, nibbling on some apple slices. "Want some?"

I pulled a couple from the bag, and then placed one into my mouth. While I chewed, I mumbled, "How'd you know?"

We settled in on talking about beauty products we liked and disliked. It wasn't unusual to find half a dozen bottles of shampoo and conditioner in each of our bathrooms, and if there was anything new out on the market, we'd both tried it. We talked about the boutique, since Monica had also worked there up until she'd moved away. It was so relaxing and just what I needed.

Then came the dreaded mention of Greg. I knew she meant well, but he just didn't do anything for me. She said she understood, and that maybe tomorrow I'd feel differently toward him.

"Yeah, maybe."

"Okay, dear. Enough with the excuses. I've been friends with you long enough to know there's something else going on and you're hiding it from me."

Monica looked at me with determined eyes, and I couldn't avoid it any longer.

"I've kind of met someone. But…it's really complicated," I began.

"Okay. And…"

"Like I said, it's really complicated."

"Are you, like, going out with him? Is he the one you mentioned to me before? The one from your class? Tell me." Monica was persistent and didn't seem to notice how serious this was to me.

"Yes, it's the same guy. As for going out with him, well, yes and no." God, how was I going to explain this? It was so complicated. "We've met up a few times." Which wasn't a lie. We *had* met at the library, but it wasn't what she was thinking or what I was trying to imply.

"Tell me about him. You're killing me."

"He's older." I paused, not sure I wanted to tell her his real age just yet. "Yes, he's older than me, so you might not like him because of that."

"How much older?" she asked. "Erica? What are you hiding from me? You know you can't keep secrets from me."

"He's just older, okay. It's not a big deal."

"Erica Jane Kennedy. Will you please stop and just answer the darn question!"

When she used my full name it was just like hearing my parents say it when I was little. She was serious, and I needed to give her an answer right then. No more excuses and beating around the bush.

"Thirty-two. Happy now? He's thirty-two, but it doesn't seem like it, okay?" I blurted out, ready to face the consequences.

"O-M-G! Erica, what does your mom say about it?"

"You're the only one who knows."

"Do what?" Monica wrinkled her forehead, confused.

"You heard me. No one knows about us yet. Besides, we're not really a couple. We're more like good friends."

"Leave it to you to pick the older guy," she teased. I wasn't smiling. I was truly in a dilemma.

"This is his last semester before he graduates. We're doing a group study project together, and that's how it all got started."

"Has he been married before since he's, you know, older?"

"No, not that I know of." I thought back to the conversation Jaime and I'd had about his life prior to coming to the prison camp, and I couldn't recall him mentioning anything about a wife or girlfriend. At one time, I'd thought he was married, or at least hiding something from me, but after I'd found out the truth about him being in prison, all my worries about him acting strangely had gone away.

"Well, that doesn't make any sense."

"What doesn't?"

"How can he be thirty-two and never married? He's not a preacher is he?" Monica tried to make a joke of it, but it was only making it harder for me to finish telling her about him.

"Hardly." I thought about the kiss we'd shared. No, he was definitely not a preacher.

"Let me see your phone. I know you've got a picture of him."

I didn't bother reaching for my phone since there wasn't a picture to share with her. I honestly hadn't thought about taking one, or if it was even feasible given all the rules.

"There aren't any," I said under my breath, and readjusted the blanket I'd tossed over my legs.

I wasn't cold, but the more I could cover myself up, the more I felt hidden from the truth. And the truth was, no matter how much it bothered me, I was attracted to someone I could never have, regardless of how old he was. Come on, let's face it. The reality of it all was Jaime wasn't someone I needed to attach myself to, regardless of how good-looking or nice he was. It just couldn't happen.

"Honey, what's wrong?" Monica got up from her recliner and came to sit next to me on the couch. "Why are you crying?"

I hadn't realized there were tears spilling over my cheeks. I reached up to brush them away.

"I just don't know what I've gotten myself into." I felt the dam break, and before long, I'd soaked an entire box of tissues.

Monica listened intently as I shared everything—and I mean everything—with her about Jaime. I could tell she was completely blown away by it all, but she remained supportive. As for any advice, she had very little to offer me. I mean, what did you tell someone who'd just confessed they had feelings for an inmate? While there wasn't anything wrong with being friends with Jaime, I seriously needed to consider what risk I was putting myself in. For now, and the future.

Before we called it a night, I told her about the time I'd worn my heels and mini skirt to class, only to find he hadn't shown up. We both laughed at the ridiculous length I'd gone to just to have him notice me.

"Now that's the Erica I know. If he makes you feel good about yourself, go ahead and dress up for him. Who are you hurting? You may be giving a couple of those guys blue balls, but there's nothing wrong with a man checking out a young, pretty lady. I bet some of those men haven't seen a nice pair of legs in a long time."

I'd truly needed to hear that from her. Instead of getting my feelings all involved, I needed to have fun with it. Share some cleavage and always keep the upper hand. Yes, that was what I needed to focus on.

That was easy for her to say, but I couldn't make any promises. In fact, I feared it was already too late.

We slept in the next morning, since we'd stayed up so late talking. I felt so much better now just having that huge weight off my chest. Dave and Greg planned to pick us up at noon and we'd eat when we got to the game.

I wondered if Monica had talked to Dave while I'd been in the shower, because Greg was a little standoffish, unlike last night. He was still friendly, but it was as if he knew he didn't stand a chance.

Arriving at our seats to watch the game, Greg took the end seat, followed by Dave, Monica, and then me. I really didn't mind, because Monica and I would probably spend most of the time talking instead of watching the game, anyway. But geez, could he be any more obvious?

A couple sat in front of us, and I couldn't help but notice how the guy kept putting his arm on the back of his girlfriend's/wife's seat. He'd make imaginary designs on her back with his finger, or squeeze her shoulder when a good play was made. She'd stand to cheer, then look down at him with a smile. It was obvious they were in love. I mean, for a guy to have his significant other with him at a football game instead of his buddies, well, that should say something. I was envious of them, for sure. Could that be me one day? Could I have what that couple shared? And could it be with someone like Jaime?

When the game was over, Dave had to go into work, so he dropped Monica and me off at her apartment. Greg ended up catching a ride with someone else he'd met up with and hadn't even bothered to say goodbye. Oh well, it didn't hurt my feelings and I was actually glad it'd worked out that way.

Chapter Nine

I GOT BACK INTO TOWN late Sunday night and was exhausted. Overall, I'd ended up having a really good time, and I promised Monica I'd try to come back in a couple more weeks for another visit. Only this time, I didn't want her to play matchmaker. She wanted me to keep her informed on any developments with Jaime, but to seriously consider not letting my heart get involved. Easy for her to say.

I didn't know if she doubted what Jaime had told me about himself, or if she felt he was just playing with my mind. No doubt, it was a delicate situation. So far, he'd done nothing to make me think he was playing games, but we're talking about a guy who'd been locked up for almost ten years. So anything was possible.

On Monday night, after my English class, I drove to the library. Just as Jaime had said, security had already returned back to normal and the guard waved me through just from seeing my school sticker in the front window.

I took a deep breath before walking inside the library. I'd chosen the casual look again tonight, wearing a long-sleeve t-shirt and khaki shorts with my favorite pair of flip-flops. My toes were painted a fluorescent pink color, and I felt confident I could keep myself on track tonight. Ray would be there and I surely didn't need to give him any more reasons to throw snide remarks at me. I'd come to the conclusion he was just jealous.

After the elevator doors opened, I spotted Jaime and Ray sitting at a nearby table. I pulled up a chair and sat across from Jaime. I took out my notes and let Ray catch me up on what they'd been working on tonight. He'd done some work on his laptop, and handed a copy of his notes to me. Jaime already had his copy, and I noticed he'd made a few notes on the side in the margin.

The first hour proved to be very productive for us, and we were more than halfway finished with the overall project. I didn't even want to think about our work being completed, since that could mean the end of our library time together.

I looked up and felt Jaime watching me. I tried to hide my smile, but couldn't. I was still getting used to his new look with the short hair, and I liked it. His foot bumped mine underneath the table and I took it to be a flirting gesture. Careful, so his boot didn't bump my toes, I left my leg propped against his.

Ray got up to go to the restroom and to return a phone call he'd missed. I waited for Jaime to stand first before I moved my leg away.

"How was your weekend?" he asked.

"I had fun, but the driving wore me out. Monica and I had a great time and I miss her already."

"Did you tell her about me?"

"Maybe."

So there we were again. Flirting. *And I'd planned to be so good tonight*. Who had I been kidding?

"Did you dream about me?"

Where in the world had that come from?

"Jaime, you're not allowed to ask that question." I batted my eyelashes, unable to resist the temptation to flirt back. I pulled my hair over my shoulder and ran my fingers through my long locks.

"Your shampoo smells almost as good as you do."

"It does, huh?" How could he smell my shampoo when I sat across the table from him?

"It drives me crazy. I thought about *you* all weekend, even if you didn't think of me."

"I may have thought about you, too, a couple times," I managed to say.

"Just a couple times?"

"Yeah, just a couple."

Where was Ray when I needed him? I hadn't planned on this kind of conversation happening tonight. Not at all. Jaime hadn't wasted any time diving right in. He knew the right words to say to stir up the little flutters I was suddenly feeling down below. It was a good thing he sat across from me, or I'd have been tempted to lean over the table and kiss him again. Thank goodness we sat out in the open for anyone to see.

Ray returned shortly, and then I excused myself. Jaime followed, too, and we each went to our own restroom. I was sure Ray watched us, just hoping he'd see something, but I was thankful Jaime didn't try anything on the way.

After I pulled my panties down, I noticed the wet spot and felt embarrassed that I'd gotten turned-on so easily. I just needed to keep reminding myself this was just for fun and nothing else. Nothing more was going to come of this.

Absolutely nothing.

That was right, absolutely nothing. There was no reason to get all worked up.

I cleaned up and then tried to dry my panties as best I could.

I walked back out and joined the guys again. I noticed Ray was packing up his things and wondered what was going on. *Was our group meeting already finished for the night?* It was still too early.

Once Ray saw me, he turned to speak. "My daughter is ill tonight and my wife needs help tending to our son. I'm sorry to have to leave so early, but I feel confident the two of you *will* handle what's left."

How arrogant could someone be?

"*We'll* be just fine," Jaime quickly added, and I knew if he'd been able to shove Ray's things into his bag any quicker for him, he would have. Who the hell did Ray think he was? This group was equal as far as I was concerned, and the three of us were ahead of schedule for the project, not behind.

"Please, don't worry about us," I tossed out, and Jaime snickered, detecting the sneer in my tone. If Ray could get cocky with me, I could do the same. I'd considered mentioning to him about abandoning us like he'd been so quick to point out before, but I bit my tongue.

It was difficult as it was to tolerate him without adding more.

No sooner had the elevator doors shut behind Ray, Jaime scooped up my things.

"Come on, follow me."

"Where're we going?"

"Shhh. Just come on."

I picked up what Jaime hadn't grabbed, and then followed him. I looked down at my watch and noticed we still had nearly an hour before the library closed. We headed to the same place we'd visited before, over in the corner hidden from anyone's view, and I dropped my things onto a chair.

Jaime immediately placed his hands underneath my jaw and lifted my face to his. "I've missed you." He planted a gentle kiss on my lips, and I let out a soft moan. How had I allowed myself to get back in this situation tonight? It was almost as if he'd cast a magical spell on me.

I didn't pull away so quickly this time, and instead rested my forehead against his. He brushed his nose against mine, and I felt his warm breath against my cheek. This wasn't supposed to be happening.

"Jaime, we can't…"

"Shhh, yes, we can," he mumbled, barely above a whisper. "We're not hurting anything."

I thought back to the conversation Monica and I'd had about Jaime, and though she warned me to have fun and not put my feelings into it, how could I not? Jaime was driving me to feel things I wasn't supposed to. And all because of a kiss. To hear him say he'd missed me only added more confusion to my already mixed-up emotions.

Without any force, Jaime guided me backward until I leaned against one of the bookshelves. I lifted my arms, wanting to reach for his face and pull him toward me again, but instead, I rested the back of my hands against the shelves just over my head, fighting the temptation. I gripped the underside of the top shelf and felt the pressure against my fingernails. It was no use. No matter how hard I tried to stop myself, I couldn't. I lifted my leg and wrapped it behind his, drawing him closer.

Our kiss was passionate, breathtaking. For someone who'd been locked away for years, he knew just the right way to tease my lips, leaving them to need more.

I loved the way he caressed my cheeks while kissing me. It made me feel needed, desirable. Jaime dropped his hands from my face and rested them on my shoulders. He gently gripped them, and I wished I'd worn something other than my long-sleeve t-shirt. I needed desperately to feel his fingertips on my skin, but it wasn't going to happen tonight with this much clothing on. His touch would surely quench the burning desire that was filtering through my skin.

No, this needed to stop. It needed to stop right now, but I couldn't resist bringing my body closer to his. That damn jumpsuit he wore prevented me from touching him the way I wanted.

Slowly, he worked his hands down, stopping just above my elbows. My nipples hardened just from the closeness of them near my breasts. I silently prayed he'd touch them. I wanted to feel him graze his fingers over my breasts, to feel my nipples through my bra, to feel how erect he'd made them.

We pulled apart for air, and I knew at that moment what it meant to desire someone. I'd had make-out sessions with guys before, and I'd even lost my virginity to Tony Cooper just to "get it over with" because everyone else had done it, but I'd never experienced what it felt like to actually desire someone. When your body reacted to them in such a way that you couldn't control it. Neither of us could take this much further than kissing or groping, considering Jaime's situation, but if this was what an older man could do to me, then I'd take him over a younger guy any day. Yes, I'd be up for the challenge.

I looked down at my watch and wished there was some way to add more time to this evening. With fifteen minutes left to spare before the library started closing for the night, it didn't leave much time for anything else to happen, which was probably a good thing.

"We need to be going," I whispered.

"Will you promise to meet me here again?" Jaime's words were powerful and full of lust.

I nodded, knowing I also wanted this moment to pick up where we'd left off. Who cared about doing schoolwork when this was so much better?

"I promise."

"Next time, wear something sexy for me. I want to be able to see more of this gorgeous body of yours." He leaned back and examined me closely, letting his fingers drift down my arm. "Your legs are sexy as hell, baby."

I felt my face redden, since no one had ever really told me my body was attractive. I knew I had a decent figure, but to actually hear someone compliment me did wonders for my ego.

The lights flickered on and off several times, indicating there was five minutes left before closing time. I leaned over to pick up my notebook and loose papers that we'd just dropped. Jaime stood behind me, and his hardness pressed against me as he, too, leaned around me to gather his things. I knew already I'd have trouble sleeping tonight. I'd replay every moment over and over in my mind and imagine what it'd be like to take this one step further. It wouldn't hurt to dream about it since nothing else could ever really come of it, or so I thought. I could have fun in my dreams pretending. Just dreams and nothing more.

We walked to the elevators, and Jaime allowed me to go ahead of him. He didn't want us to walk out side by side and give anyone the impression we'd been together, schoolwork or not. We didn't need to draw unnecessary attention to ourselves.

My car was the only one left in the front lot, and after I got in behind the wheel, I watched as Jaime stood next to the pole, waiting for the bus to arrive to take him back to the prison. He looked like any other man standing there. I noticed his jumpsuit again, something I'd gotten used to seeing him in now, and I hated that he had to wear it.

For a moment, I felt saddened. For ten years, that man had missed out on so much of his life. Yes, he should have to pay a price for the crime he'd committed, but knowing he hadn't seen his mother, brothers and sisters, or a girlfriend or wife that he could have left behind was hard to fathom. In just a couple months, he'd be facing the world with a completely new vision. He'd be a free, educated man, and I wondered if there would be any place for me in his life once that time came. I couldn't help but wonder if I was just something to help pass the time for him, or if I was truly something that turned him on.

Chapter Ten

THE NEXT AFTERNOON, BEFORE LEAVING work, I changed into something a little more revealing. The idea that Jaime had wanted me to wear something sexy tonight had given me so much more to think about. Maybe this could turn in to something fun. I'd carefully examined a few things in my closet that morning and had realized there wasn't much to pick from. If I was seriously going to start wearing something to catch his eye, I needed to do some shopping.

I managed to sneak out of the bathroom without being seen by my boss. Joann would have drilled me with questions if she'd seen the way I was dressed. I wasn't going out with my friends for a "night on the town." I was headed to class. And, mind you, dressed like I was *looking for something.*

I'd picked out a knee-length, tight black skirt and paired it with a fitted white button-up blouse. Underneath, I wore a lacy black shelf bra that gave my breasts that little bit of extra lift. I was a "C" cup, but what man didn't enjoy seeing, or in my case *feeling,* that added perkiness. I might be convinced to let him *feel* a little something, but there was no way my shirt was coming completely off. He could use his imagination for anything else and, apparently, he'd already been doing that.

I loathed women who wore colored bras underneath white garments. I thought it to be cheap and slutty-looking. This time I didn't care how it made anyone look, myself included. I was going to have fun tonight, and who knew, I might enjoy it.

My red heels clicked against the tile floor and before I'd even made it out to my car, I was already regretting wearing them. They were seriously killing my feet. Hopefully, no one would notice if I slipped them off while I sat at the table during class.

I think the security guy did a double take when I drove through the base entrance, and it gave me the bit of encouragement I needed to walk into the classroom. I couldn't tell you how many times on the way there that I'd thought about changing back into my comfortable work clothes, ones that were more me and not the image I tried to give off.

Jaime was already seated, and I thought his jaw was going to hang open permanently as I stepped in behind him and took my seat. I may have even brushed my breasts up against him just to tease him.

"Is this what you had in mind?" I leaned toward him to pull my book from my bag, giving him a glimpse of my added cleavage. I'd thought about unbuttoning the second button, but had held off. Jaime wouldn't mind the view, but I wasn't sure how the other classmates would take to my choice of attire. I didn't want to give off the image of being a slut, but it felt good to tease Jaime. Plus, it was good for my ego.

Once class started, I realized Ray wasn't in his seat yet. Don't get me wrong, I didn't mind, but it was unlike him to miss class. If he wasn't in control, he didn't like it one bit and didn't mind pointing out anyone else's weaknesses.

To say I was surprised when Professor Jordon announced that class was going to be dismissed early tonight would be an understatement. He'd had a family emergency and needed to tend to it, so we were free to work on the project or leave for the second hour of class.

Knowing the bus schedule, Jaime quickly instructed me to go on to the library and he'd meet me there soon. He had about ten minutes to wait for the bus to come back through again with the next group of inmates, and then he'd be on his way over. It would give me just enough time to freshen up in the restroom before he arrived.

Tonight was almost too good to be true. I hadn't anticipated going to the library tonight and started to have second thoughts again about what I'd chosen to wear. Did I really know what I was getting myself into? I kept telling myself to stay confident. It was, after all, just for fun.

Fun for me or fun for him?

Tell that one to my brain and *my* heart. At this point, I wasn't sure I could keep my heart from getting involved. In fact, I thought it already was and it was just too easy to pretend it wasn't. The tears I'd shed while visiting with Monica over the weekend was the sign I needed to know it was more than just my brain involved in this little game of ours. It was fun, but dangerous, too.

I walked to the back corner on the second floor and waited for Jaime to arrive. I was thankful there was hardly anyone there tonight, which was typical for this late in the evening. I found it hard to focus on anything while I waited. I was nervous but excited all at the same time.

Fifteen minutes passed, and I finally heard the sound of heavy shoes walking on the floor. I knew it was him even before he joined me.

He leaned down and kissed the side of my neck. "Hello, beautiful." Chills ran through my body.

He sat across from me at the table and I wondered what that was all about. We spent the first couple minutes talking about my day and it helped me to relax, knowing he'd inquired about more than just what was on both our minds at the moment.

"Do you know what this is doing to me tonight?" he teased as his gaze dropped to my breasts.

"It's what you wanted, right?" I asked as I tried to portray that innocent schoolgirl look on my face.

"Damn, woman. I wasn't expecting all *this*." He used his hand to point at my chest all the way down to my shoes.

When I'd visited the restroom earlier, I'd unbuttoned the next button on my blouse so he'd have no reason not to see farther down.

"You like what you see so far?" I asked in my best sultry voice.

"I'll have good dreams tonight, for sure." He grinned. "You should dress like this all the time. It makes you look older."

"Older, huh? And I thought you liked the younger look."

"Oh, I do, but this is so much more than I ever thought you'd do." He slid his leg closer so his rested against mine. My toes were so sore from the shoes. I wondered if he'd care if I took them off.

"I can't promise I'll wear these shoes again, though," I managed to bring up. "They're killing my feet."

"Let me see them," he instructed, and I slipped one of the three-inch heels off and then placed my foot against his chair between his legs. I wondered if that was what he'd been planning the whole time since he'd taken the seat across from me instead of beside me. I'd admit, I was curious as to what was running through his mind just then.

I relaxed back in my chair as he used his fingers to massage my foot. He started with my heel, then worked his way up to my arch, and then to my toes. I was thankful for the pedicure I'd gotten on Sunday while I'd been visiting Monica. I had a thing for feet and always tried to keep mine in the best condition.

He applied just the right amount of pressure to ease the soreness the shoes had caused. As he glided his fingers over my toes, my panties dampened. Was it possible to get turned-on by a foot massage? I'd read stories before, but never knew there was truth to it. I closed my eyes and imagined him doing more.

When he was finished with one foot, he slowly placed it onto the floor and then tapped his chair for me to put the other one in its place. He treated this one just as sensually as he'd done the other. I was so turned-on from his touch, I needed more. I never knew how erotic it was to have your feet massaged in all the right places. Now, I had the desire to feel his hands on other places of my body, too.

Before he was finished, he slid up to the edge of the chair and allowed my foot to rest against the hardness that had formed between his legs. I wasn't into kinky, but for him I might make an exception. It *had* been a good thing when he'd taken the seat across from me, after all, but now, I needed him closer. I needed him next to me.

Rather than wait for him to make the next move, I stood from my chair, slipped my shoes back on and walked around the table. Before I could pull out the chair beside him, he stood and reached for my hand.

"Where are we going?" I asked as he pulled me along. I trusted that Jaime knew all the "safe areas" so we wouldn't be seen.

I tiptoed carefully so I wouldn't make any noise on the part of the floor that wasn't carpeted. We stopped at an alcove area where the windows were floor-length, and he pushed me up against the glass.

"We can't be here," I told him. "Someone outside might see us."

He placed his fingers over my lips to quiet me before covering them with his own. In between his needful kisses, he mumbled. "Don't worry." More kissing. "The windows are tinted."

Now deeper kissing.

Intense kissing.

I liked this and didn't want him to stop.

He brought his lips down to the open area of my blouse. I felt the heat coming from my skin, needing him to cool me off. He sucked and nipped just above my breasts, and I thought they were going to pop free from my bra. I wanted to feel his lips there. I wanted him to suck more, to bite my nipples. I arched my back and pushed my chest out more for him.

He had to know he tortured me, and finally brought his hand up to unbutton the next button.

"Ahh. Lace. I love lots of lace." He spoke softly as he maneuvered my bra so both my breasts sprang forward. "Erica, these are so beautiful." He groped and massaged them while I yearned for him to place one of them inside his mouth.

I sucked in a deep breath as he clamped down on one nipple, holding it firmly in place with his teeth while he used his tongue to make circles on the nipple itself. I rose onto my tiptoes. The feeling was incredible and unlike any other sensation I'd ever experienced before.

He moved his mouth to share the same attention with my other breast, and it wouldn't be long before I whimpered out loud. I could barely contain myself.

Lifting my skirt, I lifted my leg close to his hip so I could wrap it around his waist. I needed to feel more of him against me. He placed his hand underneath to assist with my balance and I was able to feel the tightness in his groin area. It was swelled and so large I didn't know what to do next, having it pressed up close against me.

Struggling to keep me steady, my leg slipped, causing my shoe to fall off and hit the floor with a loud *thud*. We quickly separated, afraid someone may have heard the noise and would be on their way to investigate. I adjusted my clothes, and with trembling hands, managed to button my blouse. Jaime went one way while I went the other. We met back at our table about the same time and also just as a library assistant passed by.

I continued walking toward the restroom just so I could check my appearance. Jaime had done a number on me tonight, one that I wouldn't forget.

Glancing in the mirror, I noticed red splotches all on my neck and chest. My lipstick was smeared to the point it barely looked as if I wore any. I wished I'd grabbed my purse along the way so I could reapply it and add some color back to my face. I ran my hands underneath the cool water from the sink, and then dried them off. I placed them over my cheeks, needing to feel the coolness.

I walked inside one of the stalls and sat on the toilet. I looked down at my panties, and they were drenched. I had no idea my body could produce so many juices. Once I pulled them back up, I noticed how uncomfortable they felt. I tried to walk normally on my way out to see him again, and I hoped Jaime didn't notice.

I also hoped the librarian assistant was gone.

Once I sat, I saw Jaime had all of his notes spread across the table. I got it completely. He was pretending to be the *good* student.

"Did she say anything to you?" I asked, almost afraid to hear his answer.

"No. She walked around, but didn't stay long. Stop being so paranoid."

"That's easy for you to say. What happens if I get caught? Or you?"

"We're not, okay? Just relax."

I trusted that he wouldn't do anything to put me in harm's way. It got me thinking about how many women Jaime had been involved with since being there. He did seem to know the right places to go to so we wouldn't be seen.

"Jaime?"

"Uh-huh?"

"How many women have met you here before?"

He went silent, obviously not expecting me to ask such a question.

"Why do you ask?"

"I…I'm just curious." I stopped. "Look, it's none of my business. You don't have to answer if you don't want to." I wasn't sure why I suddenly had changed my mind. Was I scared to learn that I might not be the only one he'd shown interest in?

I stood and gathered my things. I really couldn't stand to know his answer, afraid it might not be what I wanted to hear. Something just didn't feel right anymore. Maybe I was just overly tired tonight.

It wasn't really my place to judge him or ask him about things that had happened before me. It shouldn't have any impact on me whatsoever.

None.

Then why was I suddenly so hurt?

"Erica, stop. Hold on," I heard him say as I walked off.

I prayed the elevator would hurry up to the second floor. I needed fresh air now.

Chapter Eleven

ON THE DRIVE HOME THAT night I thought about what had just happened. I looked down at my shirt that was still partially opened, and buttoned it all the way up. I felt cheap, used. Why? I wasn't exactly sure. Why was making out with Jaime any different from someone else? Was it because he was older than me? Was it because he was a prisoner?

I closed my bedroom door and then immediately removed all my clothes. Right before I tossed my top into the hamper to be washed, I lifted it to my nose. Sure enough, it smelled just like him. As I breathed in his scent, it brought tears to my eyes just thinking about it. He didn't wear any kind of cologne, or at least none that I'd detected. I seriously doubted he was even allowed to have any. The scent was just clean, manly. And it consumed me.

I really liked Jaime. He was fun to be with, and we enjoyed each other's company, the little bit we were able to actually be together. What would we be like together in the real world? Would I be so apt to throw myself at him as I'd just done if we were free to do things like ordinary couples without the rules and restrictions? Or would I be more focused and conservative, more like the real person that I am? Don't get me wrong, I enjoyed the teasing and flirting, but was it right? I couldn't help the feelings and emotions he brought out in me, even if they were a little kinky. The man just really turned me on.

I gave up the battle and decided not to worry about it anymore. It wasn't going to be solved now or even a couple months from now. The deciding factor would be once Jaime was released, would he still have an interest in me? Or would the truth be revealed when I no longer heard anything from him? I just hoped when I woke up in the morning I'd feel differently about it all.

*****

The next evening, I arrived at the library late. At one point, I'd actually contemplated if I should even come at all. I'd made up my mind I wasn't going to do anything to put myself through any more pain and anguish. At least not tonight, anyway.

The three of us worked diligently on our project, and other than one final read through, we had it nearly completed. Ray said he'd go over it in-depth one more time over the weekend, make final copies for both of us, then we'd be ready to present it to Professor Jordon. I felt confident in our work, and despite my feelings toward Ray, I was actually glad to have been placed in the group with him. He took his work seriously and didn't settle for mediocre effort. Jaime also did above average work. When we'd gotten our first test scores back, both of them had scored high A's, whereas I'd been happy with my B-plus.

Ray didn't bother to hang around once we'd called it a night, and I looked at Jaime, wondering if he planned to stay.

"Are you okay? You seem distant tonight," he said once Ray was out of earshot. I detected concern in his voice.

"I'm fine." I was short, but didn't know what more to say. I was still dealing with my emotions from earlier. Technically, we didn't owe each other anything. We were just two students who'd taken a liking to one another and had fooled around. I wouldn't get emotionally attached to him. I absolutely couldn't let that happen. *Right. Who am I kidding?*

"You don't seem fine to me. I know you left last night feeling like I was just using you. You got upset when you asked me if there had been other girls in previous classes, and I'm sorry."

"Jaime, look, it's not a big deal. I got a little carried away. That's all. It's really none of my business." *Then why was I getting all upset all over again if it was no big deal?*

"I don't want to hurt you, Erica. I like being with you. You're fun and you tease the hell out of me. I go back to camp every night wishing I could have just one night with you away from here, away from this place. Just one night."

He tossed his hands up with a look of frustration on his face. "You and I, we're different. We've got completely different backgrounds, and you deserve better than me. I have a criminal record that will stay with me for the rest of my life. It doesn't matter what I do after I leave here, certain things are part of my life and that will never change. You deserve so much more than me."

I listened intently to what he said. Yes, we did come from two totally different cultures, but it didn't mean I should judge him or hold anything against him. If he was being honest with me, and I really think he was, there was no need for me to take him for granted. He owed me nothing. If we remained friends once he left there, then that was just an added bonus. If we didn't, I could honestly say I'd enjoyed our time together. He'd truly made my first semester of college one I'd never forget. Not even Monica could compete with what I'd experienced. I just needed to stop being so serious and let things happen naturally. I needed to enjoy the ride and have fun because Jaime wasn't always going to be there.

Life was way too short.

I bit my bottom lip to hold back tears. He was right, I did deserve more. And I also believed he deserved more, too. More than what he was giving himself credit for.

He saw I was upset, so he quickly changed the subject.

"So, now that we're finishing up with our project, do you think you'd want to meet up here sometimes? You know, just to talk."

I didn't think our limited time in class was enough, and I was glad he'd asked.

"I'd love to keep coming here to see you. You're one of the few things I look forward to every day."

I couldn't hide the smile that crept onto my face through the remaining tears. Just hearing him ask gave me hope.

We spent the remainder of our time together just talking about us. I shared with him the anger and frustration I'd felt toward my parents after the divorce and how they'd altered my original plans for college. In some ways, I guessed that had been a good thing, or I would have never met Jaime.

We also discussed what it was like for him not having a father while growing up, and I suddenly felt bad for my ill feelings toward my own.

"I didn't know who I was angrier with more, my mom or dad," I told him. "I wanted to blame somebody just because they hadn't thought about my feelings. Never did I consider how they must be feeling. They kept telling me they were both sorry, but I didn't want to listen."

"Well, you are pretty stubborn," he teased.

"I am not." I reached out and playfully pushed his arm. It felt good for things to be normal again, if *normal* was even possible.

After we gathered our things to leave for the night, I stepped inside the elevator with him. I really didn't care if someone saw us together right then. We were friends, no matter what the rules said.

Before we reached the main floor, Jaime leaned over and hugged me. Honestly, it felt good to be held for those few moments, and I couldn't remember the last time someone had done that. Sometimes it was the little things that meant so much.

As I drove out of the parking lot, I waved to him. He held his hand up and a smile spread across his face.

*****

I picked up an extra shift at work over the weekend and it helped to keep my mind off Jaime. I admit, there was something deeper than what I wanted to believe, and rather than fight it, I decided I'd just see where it would take me. He didn't have to like me and he didn't have to meet up with me again, but he'd wanted to, and that was all the reassurance I needed to know there was more on his part, too.

On Tuesday night, Jaime didn't show up for class, and I was worried something may have happened to him. Had someone seen us at the library together? Had he gotten in trouble? Our presentation was coming up the following week, and the last thing that needed to happen was to lose another group member now. Why was I suddenly thinking the worst?

I became even more worried on Thursday night when Jaime didn't show up yet again. I walked to the restroom to splash cold water onto my face after the first hour had passed. I was having trouble concentrating and I hoped this would help me regain my focus. Once I walked out, a dark-skinned guy wearing one of the Falcon Club jumpsuits stepped out in front of me and I ran right into him.

"Excuse me. I didn't see you." I felt bad for not paying attention to where I was going.

"Here," he mumbled, then handed me a blank white envelope. I didn't have time to ask him who it was from or what it was about before he'd disappeared around the corner.

I took my seat again and stared at the envelope lying on the table in front of me. I tore open the back flap and then slipped out the piece of paper that was inside.

I've missed seeing you and wanted to let you know the reason I've not been to class is because I've been sick. I started feeling bad over the weekend and by Monday I was burning up with a fever. The wardens sent me to the medic and I tested positive for strep. I'm not sure where I got it from, but wanted you to know in case you started to feel ill so you'd have an idea of what it might be. I hope you don't get it, because this is some nasty stuff. I should be feeling better by next week and hope you'd like to meet at the library on Monday night. Until then, sweet dreams, my love. See you in our spot. XOXO – J

I reread his letter again and felt relieved knowing he was just sick and nothing more. I placed the note back inside the envelope and then tucked it into my purse.

We'd never talked about him having visitors at the camp, and I wondered how much trouble it'd be to see him. Did federal inmates get visitation privileges? It wasn't something I was willing to try on my own without speaking with him about it first, so I had no other choice but to wait until Monday and hope he was well enough to return to the library again.

Chapter Twelve

MONICA CAME HOME OVER THE weekend, and I was glad to see her smiling face. She and Dave were still dating, and I was happy for her. She hinted around about Jaime, but I didn't volunteer too much information. With the semester halfway over, I didn't want to think about what I was going to do when it ended.

The fair was in town, and it didn't take much for her to convince me to go. There was nothing better than smelling the candied apples and cotton candy. We walked through the exhibits inside the main building and even got to see a rodeo. We cheered at the cowboys as they rode the bulls and roped the cattle. One cowboy even spotted us up in the bleachers and tipped his hat to us. It was just like old times with Monica, and I was glad she'd talked me into going.

Once we hit the midway, we purchased armbands so we could ride all the rides over and over. Getting off the Ferris wheel, I noticed a couple who waited to take our seat. The man was obviously much older than the woman, but no one paid any attention to them. Except me. They were lovers and it showed just from the way they looked at each other, the way they stood close to one another, the way they touched. He held her hand as she took her place in the seat next to him. Then he leaned over and kissed her, not caring if anyone saw them.

"Hey. You coming?"

I hadn't realized how engrossed I'd been in the couple.

"Yeah, I'm coming."

"What was that all about? Did you know them?"

"Nope, never seen them before."

I wondered if that could be Jaime and me one day. Maybe?

We grabbed a couple corndogs, and then stopped to play a few games. Monica and I took turns throwing darts at a wall set up with balloons until we'd popped enough to get a medium-size stuffed animal. We talked the carnival guy into letting us have two smaller ones instead of just the medium one. Monica grabbed a frog with bright spots that hung overhead, and I selected an odd-looking bird that was clipped to the side of the stand.

"What the heck is that?" she questioned when she saw what I'd picked out. "You should have gotten something pretty like my frog."

She held it up to my face, and I pushed it away playfully. As many times as I'd come to the fair and played the games, I didn't think I'd ever seen anything like it.

"It's a bird of some sort, I think."

"Look at how the wings are spread apart. I think it's deformed or something." She laughed at the unattractive appearance of the stuffed animal.

"I don't know. It just sort of looks like it's soaring. It's unique."

"Let me see it," she said as she pulled it from my hands.

Tilting it to the side, she pulled at the tag on the back of the bird so she could read the small print. All those stuffed animals were made in mass quantities, no doubt from a foreign country overseas, and cost pennies to make. They seriously weren't worth much of anything and most likely ended up on a shelf somewhere to collect dust. If people were smart, they'd just go to the toy store and purchase a stuffed animal instead of paying so much money on those games. They were being ripped off with the quality of the items they won, but everyone did it. Guys emptied their wallets for that one special stuffed animal for their sweetheart. It happened all the time. You simply couldn't leave the fair without one.

"Look at this," Monica added as she did a closer examination on the stuffed bird.

"What?" I couldn't imagine what she'd found now. She checked it out so closely I wondered if she just wanted to swap.

"It says it's a falcon. Who would have guessed?"

She tossed it back over to me and we headed toward the exit. I tucked the bird tightly underneath my arm and thought of Jaime, the Falcon Club, and the emblem on his jumpsuit. I didn't know the significance of it, but I was glad I'd chosen the stuffed falcon.

Monica spent most of Sunday with her family and stopped by to tell me goodbye later that evening before she left to go back to school.

"Whatever's bugging you, you're going to be fine, you know."

She gave me a hug. I knew she was right. I hadn't told her any more, but somehow she knew. Best friends just had a way of knowing those things.

*****

The next day, I wondered if Jaime was well enough to meet. Before leaving the main campus building, I stopped in at the coffee shop and grabbed a cup of soup, a cold-cut sandwich and a bottled water. I stuffed an assortment of condiments for the sandwich into my purse and then headed to the car.

Once I arrived at the library, I noticed the bus driving off, and I quickly looked toward the entrance to see if I could spot Jaime among the other inmates who were already walking in. My heart fluttered and I took it as a good sign—he *had* to show up tonight. I needed to see him again. I wasn't able to pick him out, but he could have already made it inside and I'd just missed him.

I dumped the books out of my bag and carefully placed the soup and sandwich in the bottom. I used a couple napkins I'd grabbed to prop up the soup so it wouldn't spill. Keeping the bag upright, I toted it inside the building. There were rules about having any food or beverages inside, but I had a plan.

I stood in front of the elevator, waiting to get on. After the doors opened, I stepped inside and prayed he'd be there waiting for me. As the elevator slowly rose, I the bag trembled in my grip. Why was I nervous about seeing him? It felt as though we were meeting for the first time all over again. *Please, just let him be here.*

The elevator came to a stop, and when the doors opened, I took a step forward. Someone else was getting on at the same time I was trying to get off, and I bumped into them. I lost the hold I had on my bag and it slipped to the floor.

"Oh, excuse me," I apologized, not bothering to look up. I quickly bent down to straighten the bag, afraid the lid on the soup had come loose and spilled.

I felt silly that I'd been so preoccupied with my thoughts that I hadn't seen the other person. The table we'd previously used for class meetings with Ray sat empty, and I admitted I felt a little piece of my heart break seeing it unoccupied. Shifting the bag over to my other hand, I continued to walk toward the back.

Once I got to the table where we'd sat at before, I found it empty, too. Disappointed, I pulled out a chair and placed my bag onto the seat beside me. Since I'd emptied the contents of my bag in the car to make room for the food, I didn't have any books with me and I needed to find something to put in front of me in case someone happened to walk by. I'd look pretty stupid just sitting there with a gloomy look on my face. I pulled my phone out of my purse, but I wasn't in the mood to look through social media.

I continued to rummage through my purse, hoping to find a piece of gum or a mint, but came up empty-handed. I did manage to find a set of earbuds inside one of the zippered pockets that I'd forgotten all about. I pulled them out and then plugged them into my phone. After unlocking it, I noticed the time was only five minutes later than the last time I'd checked. I turned on the music app and then placed the buds into my ears. I scrolled through a couple songs before settling on a few of my favorites then closed my eyes and listened to the words. Once the second song came to an end, I had the strangest feeling someone stood close by. I pulled one bud out and turned around to see Jaime leaning against the bookshelf, staring at me.

"Hello, beautiful."

It was so good to hear his voice.

"How long have you been standing there?" I felt my cheeks blush.

"Not long, but long enough for me to realize I've been away from you for far too long."

Had he just said he'd been away from me for too long?

He walked over to the table, leaned down, and brushed his lips against the side of my neck. Oh yes, I had missed him, too.

"How are you feeling?" I was at a loss for words.

"Much better, thank you for asking."

I picked the bag up from the chair and offered him the seat beside me.

"What's that smell?" he asked, and I noticed him titling his head upward as though trying to figure it out.

I'd completely forgotten all about the soup and brought my bag toward me.

"Oh, I almost forgot. I brought you something. I hope it's still okay."

"It smells like food."

"Actually, it is. I figured with you being sick you might not have had much of an appetite lately, so I brought you some chicken soup. I just hope it's still warm." I unzipped the bag to pull everything out for him and quickly stopped. "Oh no."

"Baby, that's so thoughtful of you, but what's wrong?"

"Damn it. I dropped my bag when I got off the elevator and I guess the top came off. Now it's all over the bottom and on your sandwich, too." I felt horrible. The surprise I'd planned for him was a flop.

"Aww. It's okay. Let me see." Jaime took the bag from my hands and pulled out the wrapped sandwich. "This still looks fine, but I don't think the soup was so lucky. I hope it didn't ruin your bag."

"Maybe I'll just go to the restroom and try to rinse it out before it leaks everywhere. I'll be back in a minute." I stood and gathered my bag along with the now empty soup container.

I pushed open the restroom door and walked over to the row of sinks. Turning the water on, I tilted my bag sideways and allowed the remaining soup to drain into the sink. Noodles gathered at the bottom, and I scooped them up with my hands and dropped them back inside the container before tossing it all into the trash. *Well, I thought it'd been a good idea.* I reached for some paper towels to wipe out the inside, but all of the dispensers were empty. Aggravated, I turned to see about getting some tissue from one of the stalls when I noticed the paper towels hanging from the dispenser inside the handicap stall. Not sure how many towels I'd need, I picked up my bag from the sink and brought it inside the stall with me.

After I was finished wiping it out, I sat it on the floor and then tried my best to scrub the smell of chicken off my hands. The soup had smelled delicious when I'd first bought it, but now, after cleaning up the mess, the smell was too much for me. I heard the main door to the restroom open and hoped it wasn't someone needing the handicap toilet. I'd be finished in just a minute.

I looked up, and from the reflection in the mirror, I saw Jaime standing merely inches behind me.

What the hell….?

Our gazes locked and my knees weakened. When we'd first met, I'd thought his long hair was attractive on him, but now that I'd gotten used to his much shorter style, I thought it looked even better. He smiled, and I couldn't help but wonder what he was doing inside the women's restroom with me.

He turned to slide the lock on the stall door.

"What are you doing?" I whispered. "Someone might come in here."

"I…I need to do this. I need to make this right." There was a needful look on his face. A hunger, a desire.

"Do what…" I wasn't able to finish before he reached over and placed his hand underneath my chin. He tilted my mouth up toward his and brought his lips down to mine. My body responded without hesitation.

I promised myself this wouldn't happen again, but dang it, I couldn't control what I was feeling. I yearned for his touch.

Our kisses started out slow and tender, and then became more intense as the yearning increased between us. He backed me up against the wall, and I wrapped my arms around his neck, afraid to let him go.

Jaime lowered his hands to my waist, and I slowly followed along his spine with mine. He inched his fingers underneath my shirt, then worked his way up to my bra. If I'd known something like this was going to happen, I'd have worn something pretty underneath, such as the black one I'd worn before, but he'd have to settle for my simple lavender colored bra that fastened in the front.

With my shirt now pushed up around my neck, I went ahead and lifted my arms while he completely removed it. He tossed it over to the sink, and I brought my arms up to cover my chest. Why did my breasts always crave his touch?

He reached up to lift my arms away, and then unfastened the clasp of my bra. I sucked in a deep breath as the cool air caused my exposed nipples to quickly harden. Just watching him staring at me caused me to let out a whimper.

"Oh, Jaime."

"You have the most gorgeous breasts, baby."

He found my neck again with his lips and slowly made his way downward, stopping just at the top of my breasts. It was so unfair the way he teased me with all his kisses.

Arching my back and angling my breasts up toward his mouth, it was obvious I needed him to take them into it that very moment and suck them. Finally, when I couldn't take it anymore, I reached for his hands and placed them over my breasts. I noticed how warm they felt against my skin, and I brought my own up to cover his. He let me dictate what I wanted his to do, so together, we squeezed and massaged them. It was such a turn-on, and I wanted to scream out loud. I'd heard about women who screamed and thought them to be silly, but now, in the moment of desire, I could understand why they'd feel the need to do so.

Once I couldn't stand it any longer, I reached for his face and brought it down to my right breast, placing my nipple just at the edge of his mouth. He used his tongue to lick and tease it. I sincerely hoped what I was doing wasn't sending him mixed signals this time. This wasn't teasing anymore, at least not on my part. I may be young and inexperienced, but right now I'd let him do things to me that a man deeply in love does to a woman. I was confident this was what I wanted, and he definitely appeared to want it just as much, too.

With him being older, I hoped he didn't see my actions as childish. He may have been detained from the outside world for ten years, but he hadn't forgotten how to please. I enjoyed what he did to my body. The torture felt remarkable.

I reached down and grabbed hold of my breasts again, and seeing as how turned-on I was, he buried his face between them. *Thank goodness for full-sized boobs.* I pinched and rubbed my nipples, enjoying the sensation I caused. Jaime leaned back for a moment and took in the sight of me rubbing my breasts together. He was getting more turned-on by the moment. Using his hand, he shifted himself. The jumpsuit prevented me from seeing just how enlarged he was, and I couldn't stop thinking about how endowed he must be. He had to be. If the size of his arms was anything to do with the size of something else, well, you get the idea of where that was going.

I pushed my right breast upward and stuck out my tongue as far as it would extend toward my nipple. I plucked at my hardened nipples, pulling them outward as far as I could extend them before letting them bounce back. I thought about what pierced ones must feel like, if it was any more of a turn-on than just playing with them myself. I hoped he enjoyed this as much as I did.

"God, baby. You're fucking awesome. Do you know what you're doing to me right now?"

Did he know what he was doing to *me?*

My panties were probably a mess by now, and I wondered if it'd be too much for me to unbutton my shorts next. So what if I took the initiative and hinted at what I wanted him to do. I wanted him to explore my pussy, even if it meant giving him some guidance.

He leaned toward me again and kissed me fiercely. We separated for air, and I took his finger and slowly guided it inside my mouth. In and out I sucked it, and then let it "pop" when I pulled it out the last time. I couldn't help but take my other hand and slide it down between my legs. I needed relief.

All of a sudden, the main bathroom door opened and someone walked in. The moment was shattered.

I heard a whistling sound coming from whoever had entered. I heard a few noises over by the sink, and hoped they hadn't heard us.

Jaime and I shuffled around inside the stall, and he immediately stood on top the toilet and squatted. He placed his finger over his mouth for me to be quiet. The last thing I wanted was for two sets of feet to be seen from underneath the stall. I quickly fastened my bra and then pulled my shirt back on. I've never been in such a situation as this before and I couldn't think of what to do next so we wouldn't be discovered. It didn't take long to forget all about the sensations I'd been having.

From the commotion being heard over at the sink area, the person was obviously replacing the paper towels in the empty dispensers. *Well, that would surely explain them being empty earlier.*

I jumped when Jaime reached behind him and flushed the toilet, not expecting him to do something such as that. He looked silly perched over it fully clothed, but if there wasn't some kind of noise coming from inside the stall, the individual might wonder why the person inside was being so quiet. In just a few moments, the door opened again and the person walked out. I don't think I'd taken a breath the entire time.

My hands shook uncontrollably. Jaime stepped down from the toilet and then placed his arms around me.

"It's okay. They didn't know I was in here with you." His soothing words were comforting, but it didn't take away the fact we were almost busted being in there together.

"Is it safe for us to walk out of here?" I whispered.

"You go first. Go back out to your things, have a look around, and if it looks safe, go ahead and leave." He kissed me and I hoped he was right. "I'll see you tomorrow night."

"I still want to be with you," I pleaded.

"We can't. Not tonight."

I didn't want to leave like that, without giving him the goodbye he deserved, but if I wanted to get out of there without being caught, I needed to do as he'd instructed. If anyone was going to get caught, it would be him coming out of the women's restroom. He'd have a time explaining that one, but to know he'd take the chance on being caught instead of me meant so much. With weeks to go before getting released, it was definitely a risk for him. I just prayed he was able to leave the restroom unnoticed.

Chapter Thirteen

I WAS A NERVOUS WRECK the entire way home. Once I'd collected all my things, I hadn't bothered to wait for the elevator. I took the stairs and then briskly walked to the exit, not even checking to see if anyone followed me. After I made it to the car, I threw my things into the backseat and then accelerated so quickly out of the parking lot I think I may have left black marks on the pavement.

I stopped at the exit and waited for the guard to lift the gate arm for me to pass.

"Good night, ma'am."

I nodded and drove through. I constantly checked my rearview mirror in case I was being followed. Somehow, I had this in my mind. I managed to make it through several traffic lights before coming up on one that was already changing yellow. I sped up, not caring if the light changed red before I could make it through. If someone from the library had seen us and followed me out, would they have enough time to catch up to me?

I was getting worked up, and probably all for nothing, but if I'd been caught there was no telling what could happen to me. Would I be kicked out of school? Would I be in trouble with the military or government for having a relationship with an inmate? It sickened my stomach just thinking about it.

Once I was finally home and safely behind closed doors, I headed up to my room without even stopping to chat with my mom and sister. I grabbed my nightgown and a clean pair of panties, and then walked into the adjoining bathroom I shared with Beth. After making sure to lock both doors, I turned on the hot water to the shower. As I removed my clothes, I looked up to see myself in the mirror. My breasts were still swollen from where we'd both been playing with them, and there were red splotches covering my chest from where he'd sucked on them. They were merely reminders of what we'd been doing. Good reminders. Hot, panty-soaking reminders.

Sure enough, my panties were so wet the only spot I could see that was still dry was the area up around the waistband. I still had trouble fathoming how he could do something like that to me, and yet we'd never gotten any further than kissing. Okay, so *we both played with my boobs,* but it wasn't as if we'd done anything else yet. If my body reacted to him this way now, I couldn't imagine what it'd be like when something else happened. That was right, *when.*

If there was an opportunity to do more, it'd be hard for me to turn him down.

I stepped underneath the spray of the water and let the steam engulf me. I didn't feel used or dirty. In fact, I felt wanted. I felt desired. And it was a feeling I loved. I enjoyed every moment, except for the part of nearly being caught.

Using my favorite body wash, I lathered up the sponge and inhaled the aroma. I realized as I trailed it over certain parts of my body there was still a tingling excitement.

I fought the urge to satisfy myself. I wanted him to be the one to claim those sensations happening to my body. They were, after all, because of him.

*****

On Thursday, I was a bundle of nerves. I was worried someone would recognize me or I'd be called out of class and reprimanded for what had happened in the bathroom. After the first hour, when I realized no one was "coming to get me," I finally relaxed. Jaime had noticed my behavior and thought I was crazy for overreacting. He assured me if someone had seen us he wouldn't be in class right then. He would have been in trouble and I'd have already heard about it. After being in this situation with him, I could see how other guys in the Falcon Club could get a little too comfortable. Now, I could understand why Hector's friend had been so easily coerced into taking him off base. They made it too easy to be together despite what the rules stated.

Ray, Jaime, and I huddled up after class to discuss our plans for our presentation. I was saddened, knowing the group project was coming to an end. There was another group assignment coming up, one that was much smaller and required less out-of-class work, but my chances of being put in the same group with Jaime again were very slim. Knowing my luck, I'd be paired with Ray, and I didn't think I could tolerate another six weeks of his sarcasm.

"Can you meet me on Sunday?" I was surprised when Jaime asked me right as I reached the end of the sidewalk.

"Sure. I never realized you could use the library on Sundays." *Geez, why hadn't he mentioned this before now?* I wasn't sure how I felt about going back there again so soon, but if that was the only other option for seeing him now besides the class we shared, then it was a chance I'd have to take. I was just being paranoid, but the thought of seeing him again excited me and it was a chance worth taking. We didn't care about studying; we just needed to see each other.

We settled on a time, and then told each other goodnight. Sunday couldn't get there soon enough.

*****

On Friday, Joann got in a new shipment of dresses for the fall, and I let her talk me into trying one of them on. As I modeled it front of the mirror, I knew I had to have one. It reached nearly to the floor and would be cute with a pair of t-strap sandals. The silky material felt so delicate against my skin, almost as if I weren't wearing anything at all. I had a cream-colored sweater that would look perfect layered on top of the dress.

Without much thought, I knew I'd wear it to meet Jaime on Sunday. I couldn't wait to see the look on his face when he spotted me in it.

I took extra time Sunday morning, painting my nails and straightening my hair. You'd never think I was just going to the library dressed like that. Two o'clock seemed to take forever.

I noticed all the cars in the parking lot when I pulled in and wondered if meeting him was such a good idea, after all. With that many people at the library today, I wasn't sure we'd have as much privacy as we'd had at night during the week.

Once inside, I noticed entire families walking around. I'd remembered seeing a sign for a children's library and knew this was probably an area that was appreciated by all the military wives. Being stationed on base, it was nice to have an area for the kids to visit and check out books. Since the library was several floors and so massive, I figured there was probably an area designated for traditional reading material as well, but I'd never seen it. I'd only visited the area set up for research, and it alone was impressive.

I walked to the back, not knowing if Jaime was already there or not. I didn't know the bus schedule and hoped I wouldn't have to wait long to see him.

A few books were left on the table we typically used, and I wondered if they belonged to him. So far, I hadn't noticed anyone working, and I was relieved. I wondered what he might try today, if anything. Part of me wanted to go to the restroom again, but that was pushing my luck.

I sat and pulled out a few books so it'd appear I was studying. This part of the library was dead silent.

"I see you made it."

Hearing the sound of his voice, I jumped, not realizing he'd sneaked up on me.

I looked up at him with a huge grin and was surprised to see he had on a pair of light gray uniform pants and a darker gray t-shirt with the Falcon Club insignia and name across the front. Up until now, I'd only seen him in the jumpsuit. These clothes were better suited for him, even though they were government issued, too, but I was able to see more of his body. The jumpsuit had obviously hidden the best part.

I couldn't hide that I was happy to see him. "Of course. I wouldn't have missed this opportunity."

"You look very pretty."

I stood from the chair and turned around so he could see my entire outfit.

"We just got these in at work," I told him as I lifted a portion of the dress. I may have also flashed him a little bit of my leg.

"Do you normally model all of the clothes you get in at work?" he asked, and I suddenly felt a little overwhelmed. Wasn't that my intention, though? Didn't I want him to check me out?

"With my budget, I don't get to buy new things often, but it's nice to treat yourself to a new outfit every now and then."

"Well, it definitely looks good on you." He winked, and I looked away, not sure why his remark had made me uneasy.

"Why thank you."

"I have a surprise for you."

"Surprise?"

Jaime reached into the side pocket of his pants and pulled out a small envelope. Before handing it to me, he turned to look both ways, and then grabbed my hand.

"Not everyone is fortunate enough to see these."

Confused by what he meant, I took the envelope from him and turned it over. It wasn't sealed and I could tell there were pictures inside.

"What's this?" I pulled out a set of photos and my breath caught in my throat when I noticed what they were pictures of.

The first photo was of him wearing a pair of nice tan slacks, a button-up shirt, and brown loafers. His hair was still long in the photos, so I wondered how old they were. He leaned against a tree, looking off at something in the distance. There were five pictures in all.

I flipped to the second photo and in this one his hair was loose, hanging just below his shoulders. It was also an outdoor shot taken near a large cement water fountain. There were rose bushes blooming in the background and the grass surrounding the fountain was a perfect shade of green.

"Where did you get these?" I was sure the look of awe showed on my face.

"One of the guys at camp saved up enough money to buy himself a camera. Right when school had started back this semester, I asked him to take a few shots of me so I'd be able to send them to my mom. She hasn't had any photos of me the entire time I've been away, and I thought it'd be a nice surprise for her to see me wearing the outfit she'd shipped for me to wear at graduation."

"Oh, Jaime. They're gorgeous. She's going to love them."

"I hope so."

"How did you get them printed?" I asked, since I thought the guys were limited with what they could do.

"Jackson, the guy who took them, got his wife to develop them. Since we do have access to the computers, he emailed the shots to her and she mailed printed copies back for him to give to me. I just got them yesterday." He was beaming, proud of the photos of himself. And he should be. They made him look like a model and not a felon. "I hope my momma likes them."

"So you've mailed them to her already?"

"No, not yet. I need a few more stamps then I'll send them. She's supposed to be sending me some, they just haven't arrived yet."

"Can I send them for you? Please, I would love to do this for you." I could tell the thought had never occurred to him to let me do it.

"Would you mind?"

"No, not at all."

The expression on his face was priceless. My small act of kindness had surely made his day.

"How did you manage to sneak them out so you could bring them to me?"

"They don't check our pockets going out, only coming back in. I'll bring them to class Tuesday night if you're sure you wouldn't mind."

"She's going to love them."

I flipped to the last photo and my mouth dropped as I took in the sight before me. Jaime sat on the edge of the same fountain, only this time he wore nothing but a pair of work-out shorts. I was speechless. His chest was…it was…mouthwatering. There was the right amount of hair, not too much or too little. What I wouldn't give to be able to slide my hands across this chest.

"Oh, my god! Jaime, I had no idea."

"No, idea what?"

"You're so built. I know you said you worked out, but I had no idea you looked like this underneath that ridiculous jumpsuit."

"So you like them, huh?"

"I love them. I'm just not sure which one I like most. Your friend did a wonderful job of capturing just the right look."

"Will you put one of them beside your bed and think about me every night?"

"Oh, Jaime…"

"I take that as a yes?"

"Wait until I show these to Monica."

"I have another surprise for you."

Jaime helped me stand from my chair after I'd put the photos into my purse. We scooped up my things and then I followed him to the south wall of the building. I noticed a few doors that were generally open during the weeknights were now closed. I figured the staff during the week was probably different from that of the weekend. Some had nameplates on the outside, others didn't. After we'd passed four doors, I noticed the fifth one didn't have anything written on the outside of it. Jaime hesitated, looking both ways, before turning the knob.

"What's in here?" I asked, curious as to where he'd taken me. I, too, turned to look just to make sure we weren't being watched before I joined him.

"Shhh. It's a secret." He brought his finger up against his lips, and I couldn't wait to find out what he had planned for us next. So far, I'd liked his other surprises and hoped this one was just as good as the last one.

Inside, the room was completely dark. I stood still as he carefully closed the door behind us. I heard a click and assumed he'd locked it from the inside. I was scared to move since I couldn't see anything.

"Don't let go," he told me, and I gripped his hand tighter.

Taking small shuffling steps, I used my free hand and put it out in front of me to keep from running into anything while I kept my other secured in his. Where were we? Was it some kind of storage room?

When we'd taken twenty or so steps, Jaime dropped my hand and I heard the sound of something being ruffled. I stood still, not knowing what to expect. A tiny ray of light appeared between the slats of the mini-blind that was in one of the windows.

I couldn't see much of what was inside the room, but the daylight shining through shed just enough light to keep me from tripping over anything. It was some kind of storage room with boxes stacked on the floor and on a couple tables.

"Whatever you do, don't bump the blinds," he told me.

"Okay."

"These windows aren't tinted like the others. If someone outside sees the blinds moving—not that anyone would be watching them—they may realize which window this is and come to investigate. Otherwise, they won't notice the small separation in the blinds."

"Are you sure no one will come in here?"

"Just trust me." He sounded confident, and I wondered how many others had used this room before, including him. If he knew about it, then I was sure we weren't the first couple to come here.

Jaime slid over a couple boxes and made room for us to lean against one of the tables. I hadn't noticed how warm the room was when we'd first entered, but now, I was pretty sure my nerves had also played a part in the heat I was suddenly feeling.

Placing both of his hands on the sides of my face, he brought his lips down to mine. He tasted like mint, and I wondered if he'd been chewing gum. He reached down to remove my sweater, and I pressed my body against his.

There was no doubt in my mind, Jaime knew how to kiss. His lips were magical, and it'd never taken long for my body to react when we'd kissed before.

Today was different. For some reason, I was still drawn to him, but I felt differently in his presence. I wasn't wanting him to suck and nip my breasts as I'd previously wanted him to do, but instead, I wanted him to just touch me, to run his hands over my body. I wanted him to feel my curves, everything that made me a woman. I wanted to be caressed and held.

He lifted my dress while keeping his lips on mine. Once it was up around my waist, he glided his fingers over the area right below my stomach. It twitched from his touch, but the sensation was incredible. I may have initially wanted him to just hold me, but now I was glad I'd chosen to wear the lacy thong. The room was dim, but he didn't need light to see just how much of my ass was exposed. He groped every bit of it and seemed to feel no shame in doing so.

He looped his finger underneath the side string and pulled it down. I lifted my foot and stepped out of it. I hadn't expected *this* to be happening today. I may have dressed the part with my thong panties, but I seriously hadn't planned to go much further than what we'd previously done.

"You're not in any hurry are you?" he whispered in between his kisses.

"Not at all. I only want to be here with you," I murmured.

Jaime suddenly dropped to his knees, and I thought mine were going to buckle. It was a good thing I leaned back on the table or I'd surely have fallen.

I placed my hands on top of his head while he brought his lips to the area just above my clit. He kissed the spot over and over, sending sensations throughout my body I'd never felt before. He blew his warm breath onto my folds, and I was in for a wild moment of passion.

He ran one finger from the top of my clit, then down, just barely skimming over my wetness. He stopped when he reached my ass, then he retraced the same pattern only backward this time. I couldn't move. This was the greatest feeling in the world. When what's his name—I was so distracted I couldn't even think straight—had taken my virginity, it was nothing like this. *Nothing freaking comparable.* There had been no foreplay and definitely no feelings or emotions on his part.

He gently eased one finger inside me and angled it upward, finding my sweet spot. It was intense, and I was having difficulty catching my breath. Slowly moving it around in a circular pattern, he slid it in and out. Oh, so slowly, in and out while he applied pressure to my clit with his thumb.

I felt bad because he focused so much on satisfying me and I'd yet to do anything for him.

"Are you okay?" I asked, hating to interrupt the moment.

"Oh, baby, I'm doing just fine," he murmured.

He panted and moaned, and I wondered how long it'd actually been since he'd been able to make love to a woman. I knew being in prison there wasn't much privacy, but I wasn't naïve. I knew the guys took care of their "needs." Whether it was in the shower or in their beds at night, some things you couldn't overlook. For sure, he was in tune to what would satisfy my needs. If there had been anyone else that he'd brought there, I really didn't want to know about it.

When I felt I was close to reaching an orgasm, I gently pushed his face back.

"Jaime, I'm close."

"Mmm."

"But…" I couldn't finish before he placed his mouth back on the same spot again.

Working his fingers in a faster motion, the sensations quickly returned and I was seconds away from reaching my peak. Was I ready for that to happen?

I pushed myself onto my tiptoes, doing everything within me to prolong my orgasm. When I could no longer fight it, I relaxed back onto the table and lifted my hips up to his mouth. He couldn't suck fast enough. He inserted a second finger, and I cried out as an orgasm rushed throughout my body.

I panted with each thrust of his fingers, wishing they could go deeper inside. It'd been a while since I'd felt any kind of release, but it wasn't comparable to this. I placed my hands on the sides of his face and guided his mouth to the spot that craved him the most.

After the moment subsided, I relaxed, trying to catch my breath again. I thought Jaime was going to join me on the table, but instead, he stayed down on his knees with his face just inches from my exposed area.

Spreading my juices around, he placed his drenched finger into his mouth.

"You taste so sweet, baby." He made sucking noises, and I couldn't believe he'd found me so tantalizing.

I wanted to retreat, almost embarrassed that he saw me in this position even in this dim light. I wasn't "easy," but somehow he'd taken complete control over my body and I hadn't been able to refuse him. In fact, I wanted more.

I couldn't resist the urge to drop my hand and feel all the juices he'd caused to flow from my body. My pussy was slick and it easily glided over my clit. I slowly inserted the tip of my finger, working it around and feeling the swollenness.

The sensation quickly returned again and I found myself rubbing my clit faster and faster. I was seconds away from coming again. I patted my fingers against my pussy, enjoying the pleasure I created in my own body.

I kept my eyes closed and wondered what Jaime thought as he watched me pleasure myself. Once I felt my release was about to explode, I flicked my fingers until the sensation coursed its way throughout my body. I had another orgasm and the feeling was unbelievable. This was my first time having multiple ones, and wow, it felt like heaven.

When it subsided, I sat up again, feeling a little lightheaded.

"Damn, Erica. Wow."

When I noticed Jaime wasn't making any moves toward unfastening his own pants, I reached out to pull at his belt loops. While my blood was still pumping wildly, I wanted him to join me. I wanted to feel him inside me. I wasn't ready for this moment to end yet.

"Come here," I whispered, pulling him forward.

"No, baby. Not yet."

I sat up the rest of the way. "Do what? What do you mean not yet? Don't you want me?" I was confused. I thought we were in the beginning stages of taking our relationship to another level. He'd caused me to have an earth-shattering orgasm, and then I'd done something I never thought I'd ever have the courage to do in front of anyone. I'd pleasured my own self while he watched. And now he'd told me not yet.

"I do want you. More than you could ever know, but we can't. I won't do that to you here. You deserve better.

Was I hearing him right? Was he telling me he wasn't good enough? After everything we'd experienced together this semester, and today, he had the balls to tell me that now. I was confused.

"I thought—" He cut me off before I could finish.

"Look, I want you. I want to make incredible love to you, love that you deserve. Love that you've never experienced before, but this isn't the place. I won't make love to you like this. We'll be someplace better, someplace other than a storage room. I respect you so much more than that, Erica."

I tried hard to understand what he said. He was right, and I did deserve more than a storage room, but if he were true to his word, then my chances of anything else happening were pretty slim. Unless, no, that could never happen. There was no way I'd risk him leaving the base with me. I really hoped that wasn't what he was suggesting. There was no way I'd risk leaving like Hector and his girlfriend had done.

I let my dress fall back down into place and then I slipped my sandals back onto my feet. I felt funny with no underwear on and wondered if I'd be able to find them again with so little light to see by.

"I'm not trying to hurt you," Jaime pleaded. He could tell I was hurt.

"I know. I was just so worked up. I was ready to share this moment with you."

"I'm sorry, but when I make love to you for the first time, it won't be here. We may play around, but you'll be treated in the way a real woman deserves."

I had to really commend him for feeling that way. While it was hard knowing I was ready to go, I really appreciated the respect he'd just shown for me. I really doubted most of the other guys he was in camp with would have had the self-control to stop.

Jaime wrapped his arms around me and pulled me close. He rubbed my lower back, and I leaned my head against his shoulder.

"You smell so good."

"Mmm. I'm sorry."

"Sorry for what?" He leaned back and looked at me.

"I thought you were implying…you know, that you wanted to leave with me. Like you'd told me about Hector."

"No, baby. I'd never put you in that predicament. Never."

I rested my head on his shoulder again and enjoyed being held. Each time we were together, it only seemed to get better and better. To tell the truth, it was almost too good.

*****

When our afternoon had finally come to an end, I made sure I hadn't left anything behind. Well, I may have forgotten one tiny little something. Jaime had picked up my panties from the floor, and before I could take them from his hand, he'd stuffed them into his pocket.

"These are mine now."

I didn't know what to say. I'd never had anyone want to keep my panties before.

Later that night, when I sat on my bed listening to my music, I asked myself how I'd allowed myself to get in that situation in the first place. I'd never known something like that was possible. I'd never heard of the Falcon Club or any other military group, for that matter.

Why had I been drawn to Jaime in the first place and not to any of the other guys I shared a class with? I mean, there were plenty who could have easily taken his place. Guys who were able to have a "real" relationship with no secrets. But no, I had to fall for the one I couldn't have, at least not in the way I wanted.

Chapter Fourteen

JAIME HAD BROUGHT ME THE envelope addressed to his mother on Tuesday night, and I'd mailed it out first thing the following day. I didn't mind doing that for him at all, and I hoped his mother really enjoyed the photos.

Our meetings at the library during the week ceased, and we only saw each other outside the classroom now on Sundays. I wished I could have seen him more often, but Sundays were more relaxed and we weren't as pressed for time as we were during the week. Also, with the staff being different, there was less risk of being seen together. We didn't have any more risqué encounters, either, and I wondered if there were going to be any more. The attraction was still there between us, but I felt as if he was holding back because he sensed just how much I wanted him. Was he trying to spare my feelings since our time together was near the end?

The weeks were passing so quickly that before we knew it, study guides for our finals were being passed out. I shuddered just thinking the semester was practically over. During our meeting the Sunday before the Thanksgiving break, Jaime surprised me by inviting me to attend his graduation commencement ceremonies that would be held at an off-campus site downtown. He explained that because of their expense, he'd only ordered a few printed announcements and those had been for his immediate family. He hoped I understood and didn't hold it against him. Even though I would like to have had one, I understood. It was nice that the government gave the inmates the same options to purchase them just as they did for the regular students. What if…what if we didn't see each other again? What if he never came back to me once he graduated and was released?

Yes, I was beginning to worry about it because we'd not really talked about that and what would happen to us.

Just what were we, anyway? A couple? Friends? Just friends who'd shared some heated moments of passion? Was there even a chance for more? Would he come back here to see me, or would I visit him in Miami? What would my parents think if he and I did pursue something once his time was done there? Would the age be a factor? We seemed to have overcome that early on, and I'd found Jaime to be more enjoyable than guys my own age. Outside this controlled environment, would our age difference be viewed differently? And what about Jaime's incarceration? Would he be able to keep it hidden so he could function normally in society again? Or would he be seen as a threat to anyone who discovered that about him?

There were too many questions I didn't want to think about. Too many what ifs. Whether I thought about them now or later on, there were answers both of us needed to consider if, in fact, there was a chance for something more.

Jaime's graduation was being held on a Tuesday evening, and his family was expected to arrive in town the day before. His mom, along with his grandmother and oldest brother and sister, were the only family members making the trip. They'd leave the following morning after the ceremony and head back home to Miami. It wasn't much time to spend together, to celebrate such a momentous occasion, but they all knew he'd be coming home for good just days after that.

Five days before Christmas, to be exact, Jaime would be released from prison. It was a long, overdue moment for him. One he'd longed for since he'd been taken away ten years ago. He'd still be expected to report in to a halfway house type program once he got home, but he'd be free and home in time for Christmas with his family. It was sure to be a joyous celebration. I wanted to be happy for him, but somehow it only saddened me to think about it, because where did that leave us?

Thanksgiving break was the longest ten days ever. My mom cooked a small feast for us, and while I had many things I should have been thankful for, I found myself questioning why things happened the way that they had.

Rather than spend the day with my family, after we ate, I retreated up to my bedroom. I was an emotional wreck on the inside, but I somehow managed to keep it hidden from everyone. A single tear rolled down my cheek, and I pulled the covers up underneath my chin. I stared off into space, not knowing what I was going to do. It couldn't end, it couldn't be over. Time just needed to slow down.

I slid open the drawer to my nightstand and pulled out the framed photo of Jaime. I'd done just as he'd asked me to. I'd placed my favorite picture of him—the one of him in his dress clothes and not the half-naked one as I'd wanted—in a simple wooden frame. I didn't feel comfortable leaving it out on the nightstand to have my mom and sister question me, especially given the circumstances, but it was still beside me at night.

I propped it up against my pillow and stared at it. It hadn't mattered how many times I'd looked at it prior, I could never get enough of looking at that gorgeous man.

I must have fallen asleep, because I woke up well after midnight with the light still on. Rubbing my eyes, I looked over at the spot where I'd propped up the picture only to see it'd now fallen facedown onto my bed. I couldn't bring myself to look at it again. It was much too painful, so I slid it back into my drawer. Maybe tomorrow I could. Then again, maybe not. Maybe it was time I started to distance myself, for my own good, but I didn't even think that would help ease the pain.

I pulled the pillow over my head, never bothering to change into my pajamas.

*****

The second Monday night in December, I sat beside Jaime and waited patiently for Professor Jordon to pass out the final examination. In the beginning, I'd dreaded this subject more than any of the others, yet I'd found it to be the most interesting. Could it be the reason I'd ended up liking it so much was because of Jaime? I didn't really know, but I was sure he was a big part of it.

I took my time answering all the questions. Some were multiple choice, some were short answers. The final question was a short essay discussing several topics on one of the religions we'd studied that had been the most appealing to me. I carefully formed my sentences, hoping I'd ace the exam. It was extremely difficult to focus with Jaime sitting so close beside me, but I had to keep all thoughts of him blocked from my mind until I was finished. I needed a good score to maintain my A average.

All of a sudden, Jaime stood, already finished with his exam.

No, he couldn't be done before me. He needed to sit back down and wait for me to finish mine. My concentration was now completely broken from the test, and I doubted I'd be able to regain my focus again now that he was leaving.

He pushed his chair underneath the table and then handed his paper to the professor. The tip of my pencil broke from the pressure I didn't even realize I exerted on it. I looked down and saw the crumbled pieces of lead and wood on the page I was currently on. As I bent down to pull another one from my purse, I watched him look my way before he closed the door behind him.

I panicked.

We hadn't discussed where we'd meet if one of us should finish before the other. I didn't know why, but I'd just assumed we'd finish at the same time. I just knew I had to see him before he boarded the bus to head back for the night. He wouldn't leave without seeing me first. No, he couldn't.

I scribbled down the last couple sentences, not bothering to reread what I'd written. I hoped I didn't regret it later on. I just needed to find him before it was too late.

I scooped up my things and then literally bolted out the door. I looked down at my watch and saw there was still ten minutes left before the bus was due.

I quickly walked down the hallway, stopping by the break room to look for him. Unfortunately, he wasn't there waiting for me.

By the time I made it to the front door, I felt the evil stare coming from the guard at the entrance. Time was ticking and I needed to find him. The guard could just kiss my ass.

Once outside, I stopped and looked both ways before I finally spotted him at the end of the sidewalk. He stood just at the edge of the parking lot, smoking a cigarette. That area was off limits for inmates, even though Jaime was still in clear view should someone check for him.

I was shocked to see him with a cigarette in his hand and wondered why I hadn't seen him with one before. Many of the other inmates regularly stood outside, smoking, but Jaime had never been one to join them. I'd never smelled smoke on him, either.

I walked up to him and hoped he didn't see the look of frustration on my face. I was relieved to find him, but angry that he'd left without so much as waiting for me. His puff of smoke encircled us, and for a moment, I couldn't think of anything to say.

"Hey there," he said nonchalantly.

That was all he could say? *Hey there?*

"I was worried I wouldn't see you before you had to go."

"Well, you found me."

I couldn't tell what kind of remark that was supposed to be. Was he trying to blow me off, or had he been hoping to board the bus before I could make it outside? I didn't like his smartass tone at all.

"What's that supposed to mean?" I hated this tension that had suddenly formed between the two of us.

"Nothing."

"Is something wrong?" I asked. Surely *he* wasn't mad at me. Not now. What could I have possibly done to warrant his mood?

He blew out another puff of smoke and shook his head sideways. "No, I'm fine."

"What's with this?" I pointed out the cigarette he finished. I tried to laugh and make it a bit of a joke, but the expression on his face never changed. He dropped the butt onto the ground and used his shoe to mash it into the concrete. At the same time, the bus rounded the corner, heading for the stop at the front of the building. My chest tightened because that was it. This was my last time to see him before graduation, and I couldn't believe this was how we'd say goodbye.

"Just something to calm my nerves. That's all," he told me without meeting my gaze.

"Please tell me this isn't it." Tears were already welling up.

"Sunday at two. Our spot."

It was all he said before he turned and walked away to board the bus. I stood and watched as he climbed the steps and then walked down the aisle. He didn't look my way. I was hurt, but I understood. It was hard for him and he didn't want our time together to end, either. That was just his way of dealing with the pain.

Yes, his graduation was coming up in a few days, but that time would be for his family. Ten years of time that couldn't be made up in one night. I wouldn't miss it for anything in the world, even if I did have to stand off to the side in the shadows. If I had any time with him that night, it'd only be for a few moments.

Knowing he wanted to see me one more time left me feeling hopeful.

Chapter Fifteen

ON SUNDAY MORNING I TOOK a long, relaxing bubble bath. Today was the day. I was so relieved that he'd asked me to meet one last time. I took extra care in shaving my legs and making sure certain areas were neat and tidy. I'd taken to shaving myself completely bare down below several years ago and couldn't stand to be the slightest bit prickly. It may take extra time, but it was so worth it.

After I was finally finished, I toweled off and lathered my body with one of my favorite scented lotions. I was blessed with gracefully long legs, and for that, I could thank my father. I rarely saw him anymore, and I wondered if it was because I'd focused so much of my time on Jaime over the last couple months, or if my father had just lost interest in his daughters. Being part of my life, even just for a little bit, was still more than what Jaime had grown up with, and I made a promise to myself to call my dad later on that night. Maybe we could meet up for dinner next weekend.

I stopped to look at my naked reflection in the floor-length mirror that hung on the back of the bathroom door. Staring back at me was now a young woman and not just a pretty little teenage girl. I almost didn't recognize myself anymore.

As I ran my hands over my legs, making sure I hadn't missed a spot while shaving, I asked myself what man would resist these. Jaime had made himself clear that nothing was going to happen between the two of us that hadn't already happened. The library wasn't the place for such, no way at all. I did respect him for that, but there was a tiny part of me that wished I could get him to change his mind. I needed something to reassure me. I needed to know there would be something in the future for us. I wondered if there was some way I could entice him to take our relationship to the next level.

And while taking the next step didn't mean it'd really secure anything, I just somehow felt it would help me get past these next few days. There had to be a next time, there just had to be. I'd die if he didn't come back for me. Today couldn't be it.

I had a difficult time picking out the right outfit. Part of me wanted to wear something pretty, but at the same time I also wanted to look sexy and irresistible. I wanted to put him in a predicament where he couldn't say no.

I zipped up my new ankle booties and then checked out the way my ass looked in the mirror wearing my skinny jeans. Whoever had designed them was brilliant. Now, to find the perfect top. Could I pull off something that showed lots of cleavage, something that didn't require wearing a bra? Would that even be smart right now, knowing I could become an emotional wreck in just the blink of an eye? I wanted to turn him on to the point that he couldn't say no, but I didn't want to risk it all blowing up in my face, either, if he stuck to his promise. He may have taken the shyness out of me when we'd first started talking, but I didn't want him thinking I'd lost my self-worth. I still needed to be respectful of myself and not degrading.

I finally settled on a black sequined tank top with a built-in bra and layered it with a matching button-up tapered blouse. If I left the outer top completely unbuttoned, he'd have no excuse not to notice that I wasn't wearing a bra. The built-in one pressed my boobs together, adding the appearance of more cleavage than I naturally would have. On the other hand, if I kept it buttoned to just below my boobs, the way the shirt was cut and tapered to fit would also accentuate my chest. So the way I looked at it, he had no excuse not to notice. It was up to him whether he chose to act on it.

Using my curling iron, I added a couple ringlet twists to the back of my hair and secured a few of the flowing tendrils with several bobby pins. It was sexy-looking, I admit, and I hoped he'd feel the need to run his fingers through my locks.

I secured the clasp of my favorite necklace, and then sprayed a fine mist of perfume that matched the same scent as the lotion I'd used earlier. With one last look at myself in the mirror, I believed I was ready. Inside, I was a basket case and hoped this nervousness would subside once I made my way back into his arms again.

Mom and Beth had just left to go grocery shopping, so I quickly gathered up my purse and keys and then headed out to my car. Leaving while they were out of the house prevented me from having to answer a whole bunch of questions about where I was going dressed like that, or about who I was going to meet. So far, I'd been able to keep everything about Jaime a secret from my family, and that was the way I wanted it to be. At least for now, anyway. When there was more to tell, I'd share everything about him with them, but until then, he'd remain my little secret.

I backed out of the driveway with one destination in mind—the military library.

The December afternoon was dreary and the threat of rain lingered in the sky. The sun hadn't bothered to come out at all, and I just hoped the gloominess that loomed didn't have an impact on how the afternoon would turn out. I remained hopeful for us.

I entered in through the back way of the library, and when I reached out to press the elevator button for the second floor, I noticed my hands were all sweaty. I wiped them over the top part of my jeans just in case Jaime reached out to touch my hand when I arrived.

I walked to our familiar spot, but he wasn't there. I stepped over to the window and looked out. The sky had darkened even more now and I saw lightning strikes off in the distance. Any moment now it'd be pouring down rain.

Walking back, I glanced at my watch to check the time. It was ten after two already and I prayed he hadn't changed his mind about coming. He wouldn't, would he?

Not today, the last day we'd have together. No, no, no. Surely, he hadn't set me up.

I took a seat on the couch and crossed my legs. Another five minutes passed, but still there was no sign of him. I swapped positions, now throwing the other leg on top. I couldn't sit still. Suddenly, there was a loud clap of thunder and rain pelted against the windows. I jumped, not liking the way the weather had changed so quickly. The lights flickered on and off, and when the next rumble of thunder sounded, the entire library went dark.

I sat still, afraid to move. I hated being there all by myself with the power out. From behind me I heard a noise, and before I could pull out my phone to turn on the flashlight to see what it was, Jaime leaned down and kissed the side of my neck. *He was good. He was so damn good. And what perfect timing, too.*

I turned my head, hoping to find his lips in the dark. With the help of his hands, he guided my face to his, and we shared a kiss that literally left me panting. A few of the lights came back on, and we quickly pulled away from each other.

"Looks like the generator had a slight delay, huh?" He chuckled, sounding completely different than he had the other night. Gone was the sharp, tense mood from earlier.

Even though hardly a quarter of the lights were back on, it was still dim, and I preferred this over the intense brightness that the room usually had.

"Perfect timing," I quickly added.

"You look nice today," he said, complimenting my outfit.

"Thank you." I wish I could have offered him some kind of admiring comment, but the drab gray jumpsuit did nothing for his appearance. If I were him, I'd never wear that color again.

"I hope you didn't have to wait long," he told me, taking a seat beside me on the couch.

I shook my head. "Not really. I knew you'd be here eventually." I didn't really *know* that, but it was relieving knowing he hadn't stood me up as I'd feared. I didn't think my heart could have taken it if that had been the case.

"This weather is crazy, isn't it?"

I got the impression he made small talk just to avoid the subject that we'd both been avoiding. His release and our goodbye.

Don't get me wrong, I enjoyed our conversation, but at some point we had to talk about what would become of us. Next week, next month, and even next year. We had to get it out in the open. I needed to know how long it'd be before I'd hear from him again after next week. He had to give me an answer. Suddenly, all my emotions overcame me and I couldn't stop the tears that had formed in my eyes.

"Baby, what's wrong?" The compassionate sound of his voice helped me to regain my composure.

"I'm okay." I struggled, not wanting him to see me this way. I'd promised myself I wouldn't get upset, but look at me. I was crumbling to pieces. I was a complete mess.

"You're worried about us, aren't you?"

And there it was. Finally, he'd mentioned the future. He'd mentioned us.

At first, I could only nod.

"Aren't you?" I uttered, barely above a whisper.

Truth be known, I was more than worried. I was terrified. I was afraid I was going to lose him forever, and that these past few months would end up being one of those stories that I'd share with my own daughter one day when she suffered with her first broken heart. I'd tell her all about Jaime and how he'd…

I just couldn't think about it. He *wasn't* going to hurt me.

I'd admit, Jaime did look saddened, but he did a much better job of controlling his emotions than me. Men seemed to be lucky like that. And I was sure that with everything he'd gone through over the years, he'd been able to harden his heart. But right now, I needed him to look inside his heart and find me and not let me go despite what he'd been through before.

"Come here." He pulled me to him and wrapped his arms around me. He didn't even seem worried about someone walking up on us. Not anymore. "Don't get upset, please."

"Can we talk about us? What's going to happen when you're back home and I'm still here?"

"I…I don't know, Erica. I've been trying to figure this out myself."

"Don't you want to see me again?"

"I do, baby. I really do, but I have to ask, am I somebody you want to be with? To have a future with?"

If he could only read minds, then he'd know the answers to his questions. I'd thought about it nonstop for how many weeks now? Even while I slept, I couldn't escape the reality of it all.

"I'd really like to try. That is, if you still will want to see me. Although you may get back to Miami and find someone else, someone your own age. Someone you'd been with before."

"Look, baby. First of all, there was no one else before you. You're such an incredible woman with the chance to do anything you want with your life. But I don't want to hold you back from doing something you've always dreamed of doing, either. I've got a lot on my plate to deal with and it's not going to be easy these next few months. Just going back home scares the hell out of me. I've got demons that I still need to face. I've been gone for ten long years, and I've got things of my own to settle."

"So you're saying this *is* it then? That none of this meant anything to you?" I was turning angry and that wasn't what I wanted to happen. How could he throw all this away?

"No, I'm not saying that. Not at all."

"Then what are you saying? I had fun and thanks for helping me pass the time. Is that what you're telling me?" I couldn't hide the anger in my voice.

"I—I just need time. I need to get control of *my* life again. I've been locked away for ten fucking years, Erica!"

He stood and paced. I'd never heard him cuss before. He reached up to run his fingers through his hair that had already started to grow out again. I wondered which style he'd keep once he was back in his own environment.

I hated seeing him lose his composure, especially knowing I was the cause of it, but we knew this day would come. We had to face it eventually.

I bent down to pick up my purse. I couldn't take it anymore. My heart was breaking into a million pieces, and this was *not* the way I'd wanted it to end. No, I couldn't do this. I stood and just looked at him for a moment, trying to find the courage to walk away. I took a couple steps, and then stopped.

Jaime came running up behind me. He reached out and grabbed on to my shoulder, turning me around to face him. "Look at me." And before either of us could say anything more, his mouth was all over mine. He was like an animal the way he fiercely came on to me. Over and over we shared deep, intense kisses, unlike any we'd ever experienced before.

"Please don't hurt me, Jaime," I begged. "Please don't break my heart."

"Erica." He whispered my name. "It was never my intention to hurt you. Not ever. And I'm sorry. I'm just so scared. My life. Your life. This wasn't supposed to happen."

"What do you mean? It wasn't supposed to happen?"

"Erica, I love you."

"Whhh…what? What did you say?"

"I said I love you. So don't think you're the only one who's been worried sick to death about us."

"I don't know what to say."

I let him take my hand as I followed him to our secret spot in the storage room again. Once inside, I pulled out my phone and turned on the flashlight app so we'd be able to see where we were going. I was nervous and excited all at the same time. Now that we'd finally admitted our fears, I wanted to show this man just how much I cared for him, too. I just couldn't bring myself to say those three words to him yet.

Instead of going near the windows again, we went farther into the room. In the back corner I spotted a well-worn couch, but neither of us cared what kind of condition it was in. It simply didn't matter. He dropped my hand, and I placed the phone on a nearby stack of boxes. I turned off the light and waited for the glow to fade, eventually turning itself off. There was no need to use it any longer. Everything we needed to find, we'd use our hands to guide us.

Jaime fumbled with the buttons on my shirt, and I slid it off once he'd unbuttoned it all the way. He brushed his hand over my tank top, and my nipples responded to his touch. I unfastened the button on my jeans, and then stepped out of my shoes. As I pulled off my tank top, followed by my jeans, Jaime unzipped his own clothes and dropped them onto the floor. I couldn't wait to see what he looked like in normal clothes all the time. I didn't want to see it in just a picture of him. I wanted to see it forever.

He placed his hands on my shoulders, and then lowered them down to unhook the back clasp on my bra. I pressed my body into his and I was amazed at how perfectly we fitted together. It didn't take long before he bulged against my lower abdomen. Not exactly sure how

I needed to respond to that, I let my hands linger over his bare chest until I felt comfortable touching him more. He was so hard, and I wanted to rip his underwear off, but I held back. I brought my hand down even lower, trying to gain the courage to go further.

Jaime reached down and placed his hand on top of mine. I let him guide me where he wanted it to go, and then he placed it just inside his underwear. He was huge and straining against the fabric. Did I really know what I was getting into? Was I ready for this?

I attempted to push them down until finally they fell to the floor. Jaime took a seat on the couch, and I removed my panties before climbing on top and straddling him. He rubbed his fingers over my pussy, feeling the juices that had already erupted and flowed from inside me. I yearned to feel more of him—to ride him up and down.

I lifted my body, just slightly, allowing his dick to tease my pussy as he rubbed against it. It took everything within me not to shove him inside me. That was how badly I wanted to feel him. Pressure built, and I needed some kind of release.

"Are you sure you want this?" he whispered into my ear.

"Yes, I need to feel you inside me. Now."

"I don't have a condom."

"Just do it, please. Now!" I commanded. I was on birth control and that was all that I was concerned with at the moment.

Using his hand, Jaime placed the tip of his dick at my entrance and rubbed it around my opening. I was so slick we shouldn't have any trouble with him entering me other than it'd been quite a while since I'd last had sex. As he began to enter me, I felt the tightness of my walls and wondered if he'd fit. He was freaking huge just from the way he'd felt in my hands. I lifted when I felt slight pressure, and then lowered myself back down on him again. This time was much easier, but he still wasn't fully inside me yet. *Dear god, what if he couldn't go all the way in*?

As I slid up and down on his shaft, trying to allow as much of him inside as possible, I felt the sensation that built, needing to be released. He was deep in me, even hitting the top of my cervix, but there was still more of him that wasn't fully inside yet. *Damn!* It wouldn't be long before I came.

Jaime took turns biting my nipples, and I loved it. It brought out a certain wildness in me, and before long, I rode him faster. The harder he bit and pinched my nipples, the more intoxicated I became with all the feelings that coursed throughout my body. With his hands dropping to my hips now, I tossed my head back, and he had to hold me up from leaning too far. This slight change in position added more intensity. He lifted me, and then I plunged back down on top him.

Jaime slid both his thumbs down to slowly massage my clit. This sensation…was almost…more…than I could…handle. My body suddenly bucked, no longer able to fight it. I rode up and down as fast as I could, and he continued to flick his fingers more against my clit. Faster, faster. I couldn't get enough. This was the most intense orgasm I'd ever had before in my life. Before I knew it, he gripped my ass cheeks and his breathing quickened. He gripped my hips again and forced me down hard onto his cock.

"Deeper, baby. Deeper. Come on, now ride me."

He grunted each time I landed all the way down on him. Eventually, the muscles let go of their grip on him and my orgasm was over. I left him inside me and felt him slowly returning to his normal size again before finally falling out of me. He'd come, too.

With both of us now tired and covered in sweat, I rested my head on his shoulder. He held me in his arms, and it was a moment I knew I'd never forget. Neither of us said anything, and I felt his heart beating against my chest while our breathing slowly returned to normal again. I could now hear rain falling, along with the occasional rumble of thunder, and it was the most romantic sound. I'd just made love to man I'd longed for and it couldn't have been more perfect.

"Thank you." I looked toward his face, even though I couldn't see it in the darkness.

"For what? I should be thanking you."

"Thank you for making love to me."

"Well, it wasn't exactly the most appropriate spot and I did go against my promise."

"I don't care, Jaime. It was beautiful. It was incredible."

My legs cramped so I stood off the couch. I reached over to retrieve my phone again and then turned on the light so we could see to get dressed. It was important we didn't leave anything behind.

After using the light to guide us back to the door again, Jaime slowly cracked it open and peered out to make sure it was safe for us to leave

"The lights are back on," he told me. "Looks like it's all clear."

"I'm going to go get cleaned up in the bathroom, and then I'll meet you back at the table."

"Yeah, I kind of need to get cleaned up, too."

Once in the bathroom, I wiped myself off as best I could, but it was obvious I needed another bath to get rid of all the stickiness from our lovemaking. I could still smell him on me, and I couldn't deny it, I felt as if I'd conquered the world. Before leaving, I looked around and wondered if I'd ever come back to visit there again.

After I returned, I found him waiting for me with a grin. My eyes were still trying to focus in the bright light and I used that as an excuse to cover for the tears that had managed to work their way back again. Those darn tears. This was about to be it. The time for us to say goodbye.

"I'll miss you, Jaime."

"I'm already missing you, beautiful."

I reached into my purse and pulled out a piece of paper. Earlier, I'd written down every possible way to contact me—my address, phone number, work phone number, email, my name on social media sites. I didn't think I'd forgotten anything, and he'd have no excuse not to be able to get in touch with me. I rolled up the paper, fidgeting with it in my hands.

"Here, this is for you," I said as I passed it to him. "Just don't forget me. That's all I ask." I tried to offer a smile, but it was more than I could handle.

He reached down to brush away the tear that was on my cheek. "I won't forget you. I promise."

Before we parted, I jotted down his mom's phone number and address. That was all he could give me right now until he could get a phone of his own. Even though he'd be living with his mom again, he'd be reporting to a halfway house every day that would offer him assistance with adjusting to being back in the real world again. They'd even help him find a job. At least he wasn't being thrown out to roam the streets and he had a place to go. I realized it wasn't going to be easy for him, but I had confidence he'd do fine.

"I'll see you at graduation then?" I asked sort of questioningly.

"You better," he said, and I could see by the look on his face that he truly meant it. "My mom is coming to meet me on base for a short period of time before the ceremony, but I'll still have to take a bus or van down to the auditorium. I'm not allowed to ride there with her. I may be close to getting released, but the government's not going to let me out of their sight for long. Once graduation is over, I won't even get to see them again until I'm released."

"Well, I know she'll be glad to see you, even if it is only briefly."

"She'll leave the others at the hotel when she comes to see me since they still don't know why I'm here. I'll be able to see them afterward before coming back here, but it'll only be briefly during the time they're serving refreshments. And then it'll be just a matter of days before it's all over."

"Sounds nice, huh?" I tried to sound hopeful, for his sake.

"You have no idea. I've waited for this day for a long time."

"Well, I'll see you Thursday then."

He leaned down to kiss me goodbye, and even though I hated to turn and walk away, it was what I needed to do.

By the time I made it out to my car, I was drenched. From the pouring rain and the tears that continued to fall, I was a mess.

I watched as Jaime stood out by the road. It was a shame the bus couldn't pull up to the front door for him, but if he wasn't standing out by the road then no one would know he was ready to be picked up.

Not much longer and you'll be a free man, Jaime.

Chapter Sixteen

I PARKED IN THE PARKING deck since all the other lots were full. I hated coming downtown to this area, but I wouldn't miss this ceremony for the world. One day I'd be graduating from here, too, but this was a time to celebrate someone else's achievements and not my own.

My heels tapped against the concrete as I walked to the elevator that would take me down to the lobby. From there I'd go down the hallway and turn right into the auditorium. It was expected to be a large crowd since this graduating class was one of the biggest ever, and I was glad I'd gotten there in plenty of time.

There were people standing around everywhere and it was difficult making my way through. I looked in both directions, hoping to spot a glimpse of Jaime or even someone I might recognize from class. According to him, there were fifteen inmates who were graduating tonight, and surely I'd be able to pick out someone amongst this crowd.

I felt as if everyone stared at me as I walked through the hordes of people. I thought my high school graduation had been a big celebration, but it was obvious that more had come out to celebrate this huge accomplishment. For a moment, I thought maybe they stared at my outfit. I'd chosen a chevron print dress with an elastic scoop neckline. It came to my knees, and I'd worn a pair of simple black three-inch heels. To me, I didn't look any different than some of the others I'd seen tonight. Nothing about it screamed too much or excessive. As I pushed through the people, however, I realized it wasn't me they stared at. It was only a figment of my imagination. None of them knew me or who I was there to see. It was only my mind playing with my head.

Since Jaime's family was of Hispanic descent, I thought they'd be easy to pick out, but I was wrong. Being that Bishop was nationwide and on every military base in addition to their primary campus, there were all kinds of nationalities being represented today.

And even if I had been able to spot his family, there was no way I'd be able to approach them without him being there. I was pretty sure they still didn't know anything about me, and I was okay with that for now.

I could tell the people were starting to head inside the auditorium, so I filed in behind them. Disappointed I hadn't seen Jaime beforehand, I figured I'd do my best to sit at the end of an aisle so maybe I'd be able to see him when the graduates marched in. The time was drawing near to start.

I listened as person after person stood on the stage and gave speeches. I wasn't interested in what they had to say, I just wanted to see him, to hear his name announced. Finally, when the names were called, I followed along in the program that had been provided when I'd walked in. Jaime's name was listed with the School of Business and there were still a couple departments ahead of his before reaching him.

When his group stood to walk to the front, I almost didn't recognize him. He looked around, hopefully trying to spot me, but with the lighting, he wasn't having much luck. I wanted to wave so he'd see me, but because I'd had to take a seat close to the back instead of at the end of the aisle as I'd tried to do, there was no way he could find me.

As his name was announced, I fought back tears. He headed up the steps and then walked across the stage to shake hands and receive his degree from the dean. He blended in well amongst the other students, no one in the crowd knowing he'd been incarcerated for the last ten years. To them, he was just another student being recognized for his hard work.

After the last name was called, I stood and walked out of the main room. I wanted to make sure he saw me when the procession filed out and then headed down to turn in their caps and gowns. *I had to see him.*

I watched a small family standing down about ten feet from me. They consisted of an older woman, even though she probably wasn't as old as she appeared to be, who was surrounded by a young lady and a young guy, both probably in their mid to late twenties. Next to them in a wheelchair sat an even older lady who had a thin patch of hair and had a blanket thrown over her lap. This had to be his family. I knew it was them.

I kept glancing over at them, and then back to the doorway as the graduates were coming out one by one.

When the woman who I suspected as his mother brought her hands up to cover her mouth, I turned to see Jaime just a few feet from me. His eyes were focused on them until I reached out for his hand. He quickly turned to look at where the hand came from, and then we briefly made eye contact. He smiled, and it melted my heart. I was glad to finally see his face again. He continued walking past everyone and had already started to remove his gown.

I focused my attention on them once he was out of sight. If they moved, I moved, too. I didn't want to lose them, because I knew he'd find them before he found me. About ten minutes passed, and I watched his mother run up to him. She wrapped her arms around him and held on to him for the longest time before stepping back for his sister to have her turn. Then his brother shook his hand. Next, he bent down and kissed his grandmother on the cheek. Is was a beautiful sight.

I waited for the right moment to approach them, but I could only stand there and watch from afar. I wasn't sure it was right to break up that family reunion. I was so close I heard them talking to each other in Spanish. At first, I found it uncomfortable, because I didn't know what was being said, but then I reminded myself that English was Jaime's second language. I doubted his family even knew much English, much less how to speak it fluently.

I tried again to walk their way, but I just couldn't. I felt as if I spied on them, an intruder invading their privacy. Jaime looked around without really being obvious about it, and I hoped it was me he looked for.

He'd told me there would be an area set up for refreshments, and I assumed that was where they were headed when Jaime's brother started to push his grandmother's wheelchair. Still remaining discrete, I followed along.

I fell in line behind them and then picked up a small plate of mixed fruit and a plastic cup of something bubbly that I presumed was ginger ale. I took a small sip, hoping it would calm my nerves, but there was no way I could eat anything. I ended up tossing the plate of fruit into the trash and continued to sip the ginger ale while standing behind a pole that offered a direct view of them.

I came up with a plan and worked my way through the people who separated us. Once Jaime was just a few feet away, I reached up behind him and tugged on the back of his shirt. I didn't wait for him to turn around. I kept walking and crossed my fingers that he'd follow me.

I turned the corner when I reached one of the many doorways that led out of the room. I glanced back to see if he'd taken my lead, and sure enough, he was within a foot of me.

"Just keep walking," I turned to tell him.

Once the crowd of people had thinned out, I noticed a set of elevators up ahead. I walked up and pushed the button to go up. I had no idea where they went to, but I needed to see him alone one last time. It could be quite a while before I'd get to see him again and I needed something to remember until the next time. He stood beside me and patiently waited. It felt funny pretending not to know one another. When the doors opened, we both stepped inside. Not knowing which floor to go to, I pressed the button for the tenth floor. I wondered if he had noticed the message that had been taped next to it.

THIS FLOOR CLOSED FOR RENOVATIONS.

After the doors shut, we both wrapped our arms around each other, not caring if there was a camera watching us or not. He held me, and I trembled knowing our time together was drawing near the end.

Once we reached the tenth floor and the doors slid open, we stepped out into the lobby area. Sure enough, tarps hung from the ceiling and were draped everywhere. There were lots of power equipment tools lying around, as well as pieces of sheetrock propped up. Light fixtures hung from extension cords that ran up into the ceiling. There was no disputing the message left in the elevator—this floor was definitely under construction. The most important part of all was that no one was there. It was just the two of us. Alone.

Jaime pulled my face to his, and we shared a very passionate, final kiss. As we pulled apart, I looked down at his outfit. It was the same clothes he'd worn in the photograph, only this time it was real.

"You look very nice." I beamed through my tears. "And congratulations. I'm so proud of you."

"Thank you, baby. Thank you for coming to see me tonight."

"I told you I wouldn't miss this for anything."

He wrapped me in his arms again, and I just enjoyed being held. Who knew how long it was going to be before I was able to let him do that again. He kissed the top of my head, and I pulled back to look at him in the face. This was the hardest goodbye I'd ever had to have. Not even when Monica left to go to college did I feel so overwhelmed, so lonely.

"Baby, you know I need to get back to my family."

I nodded and felt bad for having pulled him away from them for so long.

"I know. I just needed to see you one more time."

"I love you, Erica. Don't you ever forget that, okay?"

I couldn't speak and had to look away. He reached for my hand and walked me back toward the elevators again. As we stood waiting for it to reach our floor, I gripped his tightly, afraid I'd never get to hold it again. I used my other hand to wipe away the tears that now streamed down my face. Once inside, neither of us said anything. Jaime pressed the button for the bottom floor, and I reached out to press the one for the parking garage. This was it.

When the doors opened for him to step out, he squeezed my hand one last time before letting go. Then he leaned over and kissed me on the cheek.

"Goodbye." I barely heard him say the words. I couldn't say anything. I was a total mess.

He stepped out, leaving me behind. He didn't look back, but went on to join his family again. As the doors started to close and he was almost out of my sight, I told him, but he didn't hear me. He couldn't.

"I love you."

I dropped to the floor and squalled like a baby.

Chapter Seventeen

I DIDN'T REALLY REMEMBER GOING home that night. The next few days were a total blur. We were busy at work with Christmas being just days away, so I was able to drown most of my sorrow in my work.

Joann noticed that something wasn't right about me and offered to run the front while I unpacked freight in the backroom. I really didn't feel much like being around people at the moment and was glad to be able to hide out away from everyone.

On the day Jaime was set to leave the military base for good, I called in sick to work. I hated calling in because Joann really needed me, but she knew I wouldn't be the best of help with the mood I'd been in lately.

"Honey, if you need to talk about whatever's bothering you, you know you can always come to me," she'd told me just two days ago.

Some things were just too painful to talk about and this was one of them. I needed time, and I needed him.

Classes were over for the semester, but the security guard didn't even hesitate to let me in when I showed him my ID for school. He waved me right on through.

I saw the prison camp once I'd made the turn onto Fullard Lane. It wasn't the first time I'd driven this way, but it'd most likely be my last. Another security gate was up ahead and I knew this was as far as I could go.

There was another entrance into the prison besides this one, but it was used for deliveries and such. I just hoped this would be the one they used and not the other one. There was parking all around, and I pulled up underneath a giant oak tree and then shut off my car. I didn't think I was ever this sad when my first pet, a dog named Rusty, had died back when I was five.

I looked down at my watch and hoped I hadn't missed it.

There was a special kind of fencing that surrounded the prison and pieces of metal paneling were woven through the chain-link fence so no one would be able to see inside. I heard the sound of the bus before it even came into view. The diesel engine was loud and couldn't be mistaken for anything else.

The gate slid open, and then the bus doors opened as it came to a stop. The security guard stepped up to them, and I watched as the guard and driver had a brief conversation. Then the doors closed before the bus pulled through.

I strained to see inside as it drove past me. With its tinted windows, it was hard to make out who was inside or even which seats were occupied. I gave it enough time to reach the end of the street, and then I cranked over my car and tried to catch up behind it.

For the next fifteen minutes, I rode behind the bus at a relatively safe distance. I always made sure there were at least five or six cars separating my car from it in case someone realized I followed it. I saw the sign announcing the airport up ahead and put on my turn signal just as the bus applied its breaks.

I'd never been to this airport before, since it was one of the smaller ones, but Jaime had explained to me that he'd fly from there and into Atlanta. With the hour difference in time and an hour layover, he'd be home in Miami later tonight. I wanted to be happy for him, I really did. After all, he deserved this.

I pulled up in one of the handicap parking spots near the front, but didn't shut off the car in case someone drove up and asked me to leave since nothing on my car indicated I was handicapped. The bus had come to a complete stop and there were two others who'd stepped off already. Jaime was the third one to finally get off, and I watched as he stood there holding his one bag.

He wore the same clothes he'd worn for his graduation. They were nice and probably one of the nicest outfits he owned. From the size of his duffel bag, there were very little personal items he'd accumulated over the last ten years. He'd probably keep it as a carry-on bag and not bother with going through the luggage ordeal.

He looked up at the sky as if this were the last time he'd take in this scenery and he needed a mental reminder of what it looked like. Memories. We'd surely made our share of them over the last few months, and I just hoped he wouldn't forget them.

Or me.

He and the other two guys walked into the airport, alone. There was no security guard or government official leading them inside. They were free men, free to go their own ways. They'd served their time.

I really wanted to jump out of my car and run inside after him, but I didn't. I wanted to keep the good memories to myself and just hoped there would be more to make in the future.

As a plane lifted from the runway, I wasn't sure if that was his flight or not, but I felt pretty confident he was on it. I watched it ascend higher and higher until I could no longer see it. I continued to watch other planes land and take off and wondered if that would be me one day. Flying to see him.

Chapter Eighteen

I'D REALLY HOPED JAIME WOULD'VE called when he'd made it safely home, but he hadn't. I was disappointed, though I'd tried to be understanding, and it only made me more depressed when I thought about it. I knew it was a difficult transition for him, one that he'd deal with for a while. It was still too early to think he'd forgotten about me.

Christmas came and went, and I still hadn't heard anything. As each day passed, I felt myself slowly slipping further away from him, but I couldn't give up just yet.

The day before New Year's, I picked up the phone and attempted to call the only number I had for him. I tried numerous times, but couldn't complete the call. It was tortuous. I didn't want this to end just as a painful memory.

Two weeks later, I was getting home from school late on a Monday night when my phone rang. I figured it was Monica wanting to talk about the latest that was going on at State. Over the holidays I'd finally confessed everything to her, and not just the parts that had made me feel good. When I'd shared his photos with her, she was honest with me and said, just based on looks alone, she would have chased after him, too.

That was the problem. No matter what Ray had said in the beginning about me throwing myself out there for Jaime or Monica's assumption that I'd chased after him, I honestly didn't. I think it was a mutual attraction that had happened between the two of us and developed over time. Sure, we'd flirted with each other, but show me two people who didn't. I felt as if our relationship had evolved into something more, and truth be known, I think we both were against it at first. God, what was I going to do with myself?

I let voicemail take the call and figured I'd call her back after I'd fixed myself something to eat.

She'd done her best to talk me into transferring to State before the next semester had started. She had it all worked out. I could live with her and she'd help me pick out the right classes I needed to take. I seriously considered it, but there was no way I could have all the paperwork for an additional student loan processed in time to start. When I'd registered for the next semester at Bishop, I'd decided against taking any classes out on base this time, even if it meant not taking a particular class that I needed. I couldn't put myself through going back out there just yet. Maybe next semester, but right now I'd settle for all my classes being at the main campus.

The microwave beeped, and I pulled out the leftover plate my mom had left for me. I grabbed a bottled water from the fridge, and then walked to my room. Using my foot, since both my hands were full, I closed the door behind me.

Since my food still needed to cool, I decided to change into a t-shirt and boxer shorts. I placed my phone beside the bathroom sink and then dialed voicemail. I turned it on speaker phone and listened to the messages while I washed off all my makeup. One of the girls from work had called while I was in class and she needed to see if I'd work her shift on Friday. The next message was nothing more than a hang-up call, and I told myself it was probably the wrong number. When the person on the other end had heard my voice and realized they'd called the wrong number, they'd hung up without saying anything. Then the final message played and I suddenly stopped what I was doing.

"Hey baby. It's me. I know you've probably been worried about me, and I hope you didn't think I'd forgotten about you. I've missed you so much and I'll just try to reach you later on. Love you."

I went numb and my body was in a complete state of shock. He'd called. He'd finally called me. I tried to get myself to breathe, but I started to hyperventilate. He'd called me and I hadn't been able to answer the stupid phone. Damn it.

Just calm down, Erica. See, you were worried for no reason. I was sure he had a legitimate reason he hadn't called and it was all going to be okay now. I kept telling myself that over and over, but for some reason, I wasn't so convinced it was all okay.

I forgot all about the food and being hungry. I picked up my phone, which was now asking me to enter commands pertaining to my voicemail. Press one to delete this message, press two to hear this message again, press three to save this message etc. etc.

I immediately pressed three to save the message, if for no other reason than to be able to replay it to listen to his voice again. I looked back through my missed calls so I could just redial his number instead of going to my dresser and pulling out the piece of paper I had written it on. I wonder why I'd never bothered to program it into my phone.

That was odd. The last call I had was from an unknown number. *What? He'd called me from an unknown number?* How could that be?

I got up and dug through my drawer until I found the folded piece of paper with his number and address. I punched in the number, and then my hands shook just from thinking about him answering. I listened to the first ring. Then after the second ring, a recording came on.

"The number you are trying to reach in no longer a working number. If you feel you have reached this message in error, please check the number and try your call again." There was a short pause and the recorded message began to play all over again. *"The number you are trying to reach…"*

To Be Continued

Now Available

Falling for Her
The Falcon Club, book two

One night.

It was one he wouldn't forget. Not for a very long time.

If ever.

In the wrong place at the wrong time. That's all it took to change things. Poor decisions made without thinking clearly.

Just as one door is closed though, another one is opened and Jaime Garcia discovers an opportunity that could change his life. Hopefully, for the better.

Just as his dream is about to become a reality, one tiny obstacle gets in his way. Or does she?

Could Erica Kennedy actually be the force that holds him together until the end? That believes in him? That never judges him?

Falling for Her is the second book in the Falcon Club series.

About the Author

Amy Stephens is a new adult/contemporary romance author. Originally from Greenville, Alabama, she now lives in Robertsdale, Alabama, just minutes from the beautiful Alabama Gulf Coast beaches, with her husband and son. She is a graduate of Troy University with a Master's in Human Resource Management. She works in retail management full-time during the day and pursues her passion for writing in her down time.

When she's not working or writing, you will find her reading, watching her favorite football team, the Auburn Tigers, her favorite baseball team, the Atlanta Braves, or watching NASCAR. She enjoys spending time with her family and friends.

Her books include Falling for Him and Falling for Her—The Falcon Club Series; Don't Turn Back, Never Look Back, and Heart of the Matter—the Coming Home series; Cooper: A Holiday Romance; and The Ride Home for Christmas.

For more information, please visit:

www.facebook.com/amystephensauthor
http://www.goodreads.com/amystephens
amystephensauthor@gmail.com
www.twitter.com/astephensauthor